Fatherhood for Fuckheads

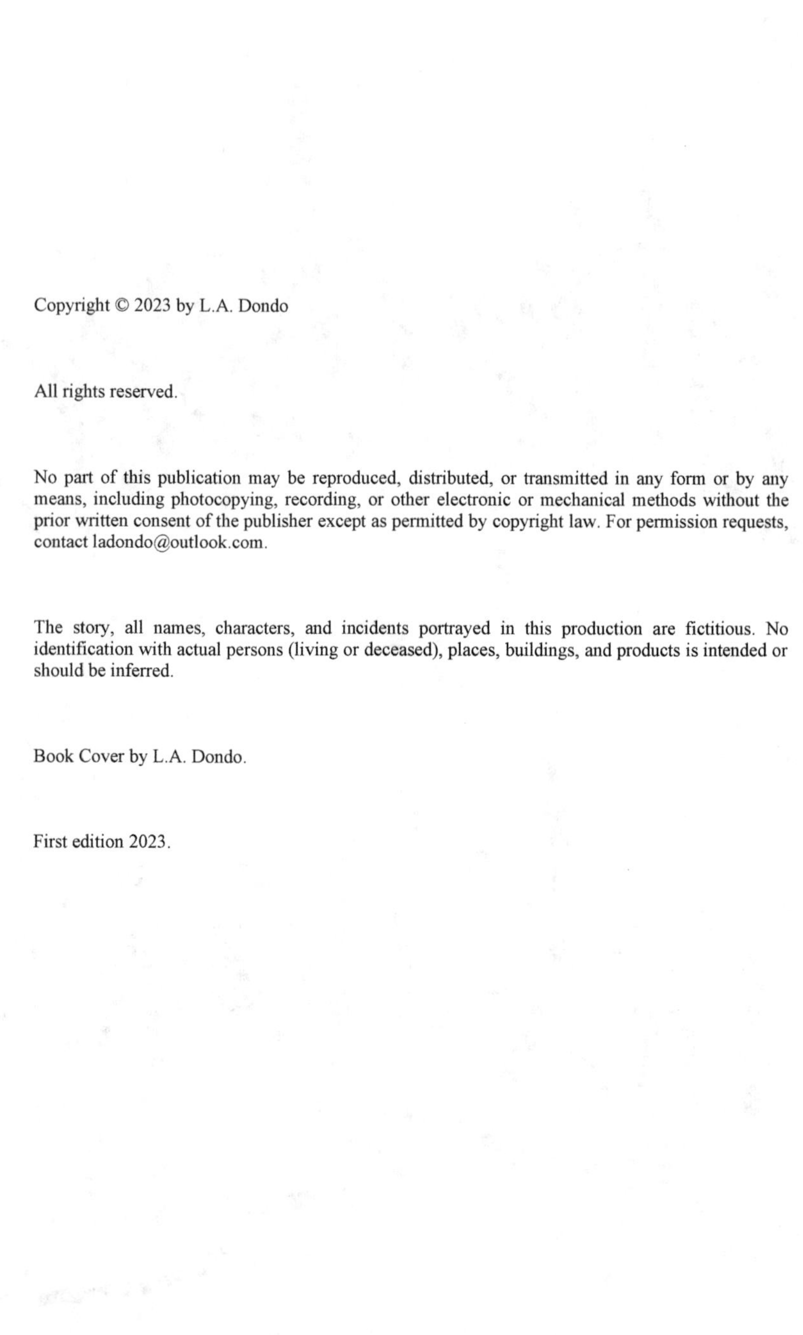

Book Cover by L.A. Dondo.

First edition 2023.

For Sam and Marlowe

FATHERHOOD FOR FUCKHEADS

By:

L.A. Dondo

Pump pump squirt.

NINE MONTHS LATER

Boris.

ONE

Congratulations Fuckhead, you just changed your life. For the better? Probably, but you'll just have to wait until Boris is out of his diapers and the moment you're allowed to reclaim your wife's plump jugs. Don't those feeders look delicious? Shoot, man. What's in them tastes like armpits though, so there's that. You get the leftovers, and the leftovers are skint.

So, you're a dad—who woulda thought, guy. Definitely not me. Would it bother you to know that I had different plans for you? A couple weekends from now, before this entire baby-thing began—pregnancy and all—I'd intended for you to be out on a road trip with the boys, but alas, things have changed, son. You got a phone right? Acclimate yourself with the best free porno there is and get used to sexually manipulating yourself in the bathroom—learn to master the art of leaving the pooper stinking as though you actually let one fly. Remember to flush or else face questions like:

"Why's your face so red?"

"Big shit," you'd say.

"I didn't hear you flush."

And it's at that moment you know your wife knows you just had your cock in your hands and you were working it like you were thirteen again and shooting pearly ropes to the thought of Kendra Wilkinson and the other two Girls Next Door and smiling Jack-Nicholson-wide, your fingers peeling apart like they're webbed. Yikes!

Golly is it ever strange to see you holding that thing. Fragile, eh? Kinda scary to know that thing in your hands *needs* you to survive, and bucko, your wife needs you too. Sometimes it'll seem like she's got it—and the chances say she'll *tell* you she's got it—but it's on you to man-up and find a way to *be* there without really declaring that you're there. Make sense? It's not supposed to. Fatherhood's a riddle that some men just don't solve; fatherhood's a riddle not intended for every man to experience; some men just don't care enough to solve that riddle, and that's a goddamn shame because where's the fun in that? Would you *rather* be on a road trip with the boys seeking out holes to put your thingy in? If so, nobody's stopping you—just be aware of what you're leaving behind. Look at your wife, who just fired Boris out her front-can and ripped her precious taint; look at Boris and his misshapen head. Aren't they fucking beautiful? What you're looking at right now is the pinnacle of beautiful things despite all the blood and sweat and feces and wailing.

Truth.

Let's talk about your wife.

Tough bitch, huh?

Have you ever tried fentanyl or oxycodone? If you haven't, fuckin' give it a whirl, man.

But about your wife:

She's blasted outta her skull on a cocktail of intravenous opiates and the first thing she did once Boris completed his journey out the womb and through the vaginal canal like an eight-pound misplaced shit was eagerly grab him from the nurse's hands to give him a big ol' hug, staining her hospital smock with colourful bits and bobs and odds and ends from the unreachable depths of her pulverized cooter. Note: your wife asked for neither more drugs or a beer, and she *definitely* didn't get up and dance. As a matter of fact, Boris's birth has sobered her entirely lo there you stand all woozy and such with that bottle of Macallan 12-Year you got in your hospital bag so heavy on your mind it hurts; you're jacked to bust down to your buddies and your father and your father-in-law to smoke some cigars and to enjoy a couple whiskies—

Straighten your back, say nothing, and just watch, fucker; you can only be somewhere for the first time once and this a moment you'll never forget and a moment not everybody's blessed to ever experience so *fall into it*, and when the moment's right, when the room is quiet and the apple of your eye, so tired, is quiet herself, lean over and tell your wife,

"I love you,"

And smile through the night and into the rest of your life and beyond into a blessed forever.

TWO

It's going to feel weird as father, being there more so than actually doing anything—at least for the first while. You're not going to let Boris suckle of *your* titty…or are you? I hope not, you fucking pervert.

You'll sleep, unlike your wife, so make the most of it because it's in this stage where you exert effort in attempt to match what your wife's been through for the past nine months, so hopefully your pals understand what's going on, and if not, it's on you, Fuckhead, to remind them that there are more important things in your life than golf and professional sports and recreational activities and fishing and crushing a few beers when you get home from work.

Moderation, Fuckhead. Moderation.

Have that beer, sure; watch some sports, hell yeah; *definitely* keep in touch with your pals—

But *be there.*

Your job is to *be there.*

But oh how your cell phone daintily chimes, its screen aglow with a fresh notification. Harold.

What a good guy, that Harold guy; a real stand-up guy, that Harold guy. A while back he gifted you and Wifey a nice bottle of Shiraz and a $250 gift card to one of the town's best steakhouses. Like I said: what a good guy, that Harold guy.

"Extra ticket to The Dropkick Murphys," you say to your wife. Boris lay slumbering in some sort of sitting-device that moves him around in a circle. He's wearing yellow socks and a hat that looks like the tip of a textile condom.

Your wife smiles and says, "Go." She's got this.

So you go. It feels odd being out of the house; it feels as though the world is tilted backwards and you're constantly falling in reverse towards something heavier and more significant, which is very much the case. Beer tastes different; you refuse Harold's generous offer of a hit from his marijuana cigarette; you avert your gaze from the dark-haired and petite-but-large-chested-and-wide-thighed stunner who wears a short kilt which exposes her buttocks with each subsequent hop. You'd rather be home yet you're having fun.

Hm.

At home:

When you get there, slumbering on the sofa is your world. Aromatics of sweaty diapers and musty laundry fill the room. Your wife ordered a pizza, Hawaiian, and it sits at room-temperature on the coffee table. Your wife was watching Gilmore Girls. How nice.

You help yourself to a slice and put on the first episode of Breaking Bad. This is your seventh time through the series.

Fuck, what a good show.

Boris coos around the half-hour mark and your wife immediately stirs. “Why aren’t you in bed?” she asks.

“Wanted to watch some TV,” you reply. Your wife heaves out a gargantuan melon which wobbles hither and thither across her colostrum-stained muumuu. You start thinking you gotta go to the washroom to take a *shit,* but you don’t so little as feel the need to fart.

Boris starts to feed.

Throb.

Throb.

You say to your wife, “Gotta let one fly.”

Throb.

“We don’t have any birds,” she says.

"Gotta shit," you clarify.

Throb.

"It's 1:30 AM," your wife counters, eyeing you with an abundance of suspicion.

You tell your wife, "Ah, you know what: it can wait until morning."

You jack-it in bed instead as you maintain your eyes snowglobe-wide on the door in case Wifey's lucky enough to get a couple hours' rest in the spot she's worn in over the years which slowly begins returning to its factory state.

THREE

You'd think Boris follows a diet of mustard given that his dumps are yellow and not unlike the texture of a fine dijon. You begin thinking fondly of hot dogs, but you don't have any buns.

Fuck.

You secure Boris's diaper and he musters a laugh that may have been a cry for help but you can't tell the difference—everything sounds the same, except when he's sad. When he's sad his cries penetrate your eardrums and send your hammer thrumming until all you see is white, standing idly—this is the antithesis of tranquil, you think. You carry Boris to the couch and you sit. Today it's just to two of you, for Wifey's out with the mother-in-law—a deserved break. They went out to lunch is all, and they left you the car.

"Run to the grocery store if you get the time," your wife told you. "We need some bread."

Driving alone with a baby in the car is as about as frightening as it gets.

You and your boy are frozen to the couch, he with a bottle of milk which he drinks, bemused because it's not the conventional delivery device, and you with your ninth cup of coffee. Your stomach rumbles often and you know it's not the happiest at being filled with such a copious amount of diuretic. Your stomach rumbles again. Boris's suckles peter-out, and milk leaks from the corner of his mouth and down his cheek. You wipe it. This is the first time you taste your wife's product and you immediately never want to ever stick your dick in her ever again ever—never ever ever.

Your stomach rumbles.

You think of you wife's cans.

Throb.

But this time you actually have to send one home and whatever's about to depart your sphincter is impatient and won't wait at the station for long—it'll sooner throw itself onto the tracks before being told to wait so little as one more time.

Boris sleeps, you attempt to move him to his curious sleep contraption but he stirs, cries, and you soothe him with the help of a soother nearly the size of his face.

Boris sleeps.

Your stomach rumbles.

Yada yada yada,

Fuckin'

Yada.

Your stomach rumbles.

Here it comes:

A poop of your own and you can practically smell it. It smells like Chipotle Tabasco.

Thank the coffee. Thank your wife's breast milk. Together they've merged into an odious *something*.

Shift upon the sofa, clench your ass as tight as she goes as Boris whimpers and shuffles; you're a part of his nap now, you're an extension of his consciousness and should you pry yourself apart from him, there goes the nap. There goes silence. There go these moments of freedom even though you'll never be your own again.

You shuffle. You fart—

Thank *God* it's just a fart. It reeks like week-old death.

Your stomach rumbles.

"All right," you whisper, standing while simultaneously pressing Boris tight to your chest so as to prevent him from feeling any semblance of separation. Boris doesn't like being alone—not yet, at least.

Success. You stand. You fart. You cross your legs like a flattered schoolgirl because the train's leaving the fuckin' station. "All aboard!" calls the Conductor, and the train sounds its whistle. *Choo-choo!*

Waddle. Waddle. Waddle.

Speed-waddle with your butthole puckering, yawning, waving good-bye to the poo which is beginning to depart.

With a single hand you tug down your sweats and you feel a slippery substance ooze. You run your hand along your waistband so you can pull your sweats down over your ass.

"Fuckfuckfuckfuckfuckfuckfuckfuck," you whisper—laughing, too, believe it or not—and you're shitting in a dark bathroom before you're upon the porcelain, but your dump strikes true.

Five-pounds lighter, you feel like there's a renewed brilliance to the world despite the fetid smell. You feel as though you're fresh from the shower and shaved from the eyebrows down. You're an Olympic swimmer.

Plop.

And you're taking home the Gold.

Plop.

And you got the World-Record to boot, motherfucker. Hooray!

"We did it, buddy," you say to Boris who slumbers. You laugh a little and swear you see him smile, too—he's dreaming, how cute. What a handsome devil your son is, truly. Your cell phone dings from the living room but it's the least of your concerns because you remember that you have to wipe. You're left-handed. Boris is nuzzled into your chest, his bottom resting in your ass-wiping hand, leaving the job to its non-dominant colleague.

Good luck.

Unfurling the toilet paper roll is struggle enough. You recognize that what's in the toilet bowl has left its mark on your bumcheeks, so you load your hand with ten sheets or thereabouts—you failed to turn on the lights so you give it your best shot. You give the papers a tug but the roll unfurls five-fold what you intended to grab. Your wife will be on your case about the waste. You work your thumb and index finger along the seam which binds the sheets. You separate a significant chunk—it's like you're holding a potato, if, of course, the potato was three-ply and cost on average about $2 per.

Boris shuffles, coos when you hoist your ass from the seat. You draw a deep breath in preparation, ready to feel your left-behinds smear across your right buttock like you're spreading cream cheese over an everything bagel.

Into the crack you go, getting to work. Yuck. Whatever's down there, it's gluey—

You hesitate, draw your hand back to collect your thoughts—to strategize.

You have an idea.

You push three fingers into the toilet paper so as to form a small scooper in your hand—like a garden trowel—and poke the top of your taint with these fingers and slowly draw them back through the leftovers, over your asshole, through the muck as though shoveling moist earth. One scoop through you withdraw your hand to investigate what it has been up to down there.

The base of your thumb is laden with poo.

Panicked, you chuck the loaded Charmin to your left, into the bathtub, and it clings with a clap to the tiles. Your shit, you think, would make an excellent spackling paste. It's a shame that the colour is far from appealing.

You tear some more Charmin from the roll.

Boris coos.

"Shh," you shush, your breath catching when you inhale.

Sloppily you wipe again, and again until the toilet paper draws minimal filth—you decide you'll borrow one of Boris's wipes once through with this ordeal. Your sloppiness marred your ham to your hip, and you wipe and wipe with vigor your employer would love outta you but will never get because *fuck* your employer.

Thirty sheets later the paper comes from your buttocks unblemished. Excellent, you think. Excellent, this'll do just fine.

You stand, fight with your sweats to get them up around your waist once again. Boris is lucky he won't recall this. Afterall, you were successful in letting him sleep through it all. You spin the tap with your soiled hand, cup your hand around the soap dispenser while plunging it downward all the while and you wash your one hand by rubbing your fingers along the same palm on repeat until you've worked up a lather and the soap is totally rinsed. You turn off the tap, dry your hand on your pants. You have the decency to turn on the exhaust fan. Good for you.

On the couch:

You lay supine, kick your feet up, adjust the TV's volume. Breaking Bad, again. You're in the middle of the first season. Eventually, you nod off, oblivious to the goings-on of the world and there's absolutely nothing wrong with that. You're allowed to sleep, especially as a parent.

An unknown quantity of minutes later, the door opens and your wife enters silently, she removes her shoes silently, and she places the groceries in the kitchen, yes, silently. You know *she* knows you're not *actually* asleep anymore, but you pretend you're sleeping because you'd like to relish a few more minutes in a beautiful moment that was bound to come to an end no matter what, but you don't want to accept that. No big deal.

Your wife approaches, kisses Boris on the cheek and whispers in your ear, “I’m going to take a bath.”

“Right,” you say, you yawn, you rub your eyes with your available hand and close your eyes yet again as your wife’s footsteps sound in retreat.

The bathroom door closes and then comes the shriek.

It goes like this:

“WHAT THE FUCK!?!?!?”

Boris rises with a clamour, immediately begins crying.

“What is it?” you ask your darling wife, blearily stumbling to the bathroom through the grog which accompanies mid-afternoon naps with your head tilted at an awkward angle fully expecting to enter the bathroom to discover a mouse or a rat or…*fuck*, you think.

An alligator.

You enter the bathroom and see your shitty toilet paper still clung to the tiles.

It hadn’t moved an inch.

Just like spackle, you think.

FOUR

At one month old Boris ere does more than sit and stare at you with gormless eyes. He sees about the length of your shoe and his peepers flitter around like blind sparrows. His head's the shape of a potato and his neck has the integrity of a warm Twizzler. After feeding, when burping him, you hold his slight chin in your hand and his eyes go wide until warmly he spits-up into your palm, and the warmth spreads down your wrist. You're reminded of the taste of your wife's acrid mom-sauce. "Sorry," you say to your boy, hoping he understands why he can eat nothing more than *milk*, or whatever this nasty knock-off can go as. You'll be grilling steaks with him before you know it. "And drinking beer," you add. Hm, a beer sounds nice. It's 2:00 PM—a Saturday; your wife's napping, you got Breaking Bad on the TV—already starting the third season.

You can practically taste the bite of the hops.

"Urkle."

Cute. Boris's first word.

"Arkle."

"Not bad, son," says you. You pat him on the bottom, lean back into the sofa. Fart. You believe Boris smiles. He did, but only because he's filling his two-pound diaper with another eight-ounces. You can hear it, it's almost like his penis is whispering.

It is.

It's saying, "Change my fucking diaper, guy. It's been, like, four hours."

Boris no longer puts up a fight when you change him. It took a couple weeks of conflicting ideas, yeah, but then you and your wife figured out the wonders of the classic tune *Row Row Row Your Boat,* or whatever the hell it's formally called.

"Row, row, row your—"

"Urkle."

"*Boat.*"

"Arkle."

"*Gently down the—*"

"aaaaaaa!"

"streaaaaammm.

"Merrily merrily merrily—"

"Urkle."

"*Life is but a—*"

"Arkle."

"*Biiiiiitttccccchhhhhh!*"

Boris laughs at your alternative but your wife, who stands in the threshold between the living room and the hallway off of which the bedrooms stem, has her reservations.

She clicks her tongue, says, "Husband," but she actually says your name which I won't mention because it's stupid and I'll help you preserve what minimal dignity of yours remains. Dads have to be taken seriously, you know, and you already drive a 2009 Dodge Caliber. It's orange.

You say, "Wife," like it's 1955; like you're eagerly awaiting lunch. She adjusts the recently applied diaper, asks if you pulled anything out for dinner. You didn't. Your wife does the job for you, which is fitting because she'll be the one cooking. You may or may not help with the dishes—the week at work was a long one and you always mix up the cutlery drawer, blending fork and spoon and knife and other assorted kitcheree into a minestrone of small kitchen utilities.

Your wife plops on the chaise lounger next to the window, mentions Breaking Bad and that she doesn't see how someone can watch a show as many times as you've watched this one.

"It's a masterpiece," you say. You're able to anticipate a good 80% of every line spoken, and you'd very much like a pair of bodacious subwoofers for yourself. You'll take a hard pass on the meth, though. You're impartial to Walter White's riches.

Your wife just rolls her eyes. She's wearing a baggy white t-shirt and a pair of shorts riddled with holes. You love her. You're thankful for her. You get up to take a shower at the end of the episode and bring a beer with you.

What beats a shower beer?

Well, shower blowjobs aren't bad, but on that there's plenty of room for improvement.

A shower beer is never dry, for one; you don't have to imagine you're force-feeding your wife water as though you're farming her for fois gras, for seconds. You don't have to your sonorous moans echoing through the bathroom, for thirds.

Ah, shit. You're masturbating again.

See: first chapter.

See: paragraph three.

You make sure to cum down the drain and not on the tiles because you're still embarrassed from the whole Shit-Incident, and surely

Wifey can spot the difference between a streak of Pantene and a semen rope. You wash your hair; you wash your body; you drink your beer; you stand in the shower because it'll be the same outside the bathroom as it was before you went *into* the bathroom. You think about work—you're not supposed to do this—and feel weird about doing this because it's Saturday and you're not the happiest at your job. You scroll your phone, send a text to your mother, watch various YouTube videos, Google random shit. Forty-five minutes have passed. You can smell the chicken.

Out of the bathroom you come, shaved, soaped, spick and span. A cast iron pan sizzles stovetop and you're delighted to see your wife enjoying a whisky in a glass full of ice. You can smell it blending with the chicken. You pour yourself to a dram, neat. You add ice cubes too, to the detriment of your ego.

A 2009 Dodge Caliber, orange.

You drink your whisky hastily and pour a second, this time with *just a splash* of lukewarm water. Boris is sleeping, again, in his curious sleep contraption.

"Love you, dear," you say to your wife.

"Love you, too."

That was Saturday.

FIVE

This is where I introduce the bad guy; the villain; the antagonist; the enemy; the adversary.

It's you, Jabroni.

See, there are a lot of elements of parenting which go unknown until you actually *become* a parent, among them being the importance of earplugs; the blending together of the first six months; the odourless shit-mittens and the indescribable noise of them being filled; oven timers….

But what nobody tells you is that you are your own worst enemy.

Home-invaders be damned; tailgating driver? Fuck 'em, change lanes, divert; Grapes? Slice 'em, bro; Hot dogs? You shouldn't be eating hot dogs unless you're at the ballpark or a barbecue where the host is too cheap to buy good bratwurst.

But you?

Nah, you're the tough nut to crack, Jack; you're a potential chink and your family's the chain; you're the wrench and your wife and child are the plans.

Let's call the bad guy Ken, shall we? Ken, because that's a supremely douchey name and at times we all think of ourselves as plastic fucks who can attain women with 12" waists and double-Ds when none of us are any more than fuckheads—

But it's Monday and we're out of the house while your wife and child are at home doing exactly what they did on Saturday but only with the extra breathing-room given that there's one less body occupying otherwise useless living-space because all a mother needs is an unfathomable measure of patience—everything else, from the floor to the ceiling and the furniture and the TV and books and sunny days, they're just extra.

Ken says *Hello.*

You say *Hi.*

And you drive your 2009 Dodge Caliber like it's orange.

Ken reminds you that you could've bought the Charger.

You tell Ken that you know, and you turn up the radio, think a bit about Boris, your wife.

Work:

That's it, that's all. Work's the place you go to work and make money and go home once your eight hours are through. You get Overtime once in a while but you don't take it often. You don't much enjoy work, as work's just a job and a job's just that—there are plenty of jobs out there and you're of the generation where you'll go through dozens before you *retire,* or so promises your government, and about them you have your reservations. Your workplace has its fair share of company-people, lovers of the bullshit touted at morning meetings, lovers of serving the populous and taking gripe when needed because it's their job to *serve the public;* to make folks happy, and to *smile.*

Nah, you think, frowning through the front door of the Dispatch Office air-conditioned to an autumnal 60°. You wore shorts; your leg hairs stand on end and you feel your nipples dig into your polyester shirtfront—thank God for your short-sleeved button-up, somebody would lose an eye if you didn't have that there.

Your boss bids you Good morning.

You bid her Good morning in return.

Your boss wants to know how it's going.

It's going fine, because why the fuck would you tell the bitch otherwise? You don't much want to have further conversation because neither of you really cares about the other, so why pretend?

Decency, as per societal standards. That's the answer.

Decency.

Right.

Decency.

You breathe once the Head Cheese is gone, and your office is quiet—*so* quiet. You can hear Ken clearly here.

Ken tells you that you should buy a gram from Diane.

You tell Ken that you shouldn't. "Plus," you go on. "I gotta hit the road soon."

You water the city's boulevards for a living—you're a Driver, and a young kid or two sit in the back and shoot water from a 55-gallon pail onto shrubbery, aiming to make everything more colourful. There's nothing wrong with colourful. There's also nothing wrong with your job because it pays $75,000 a year. Ken would have rather had you stay at your former line cook job, plonking waitresses in the Walk-In during the lulls in a dinner rush, though.

Ken asks if you remember Muriel.

Hell yeah you do! Though unfortunately, she's the one that got away. Muriel and her formidable tookus.

Lotta acne, though, you tell Ken.

Ken likes 'em so long as they're willing.

You, a man of reason, ignore Ken. You don't want to get Ken angry. When Ken gets angry, he gets loud, so you tuck him into the back of your mind and tell him to stay there until the day is done.

You've got a lot of plants to water and a truck to drive. Shit. There's no time for Ken.

Grab the keys; hear them jingle, they're heavy—maybe a pound and a half altogether. There's about thirty keys on the key ring but you only use four: one for the truck, one for the Transit bathrooms located at various bus stops, one for the pumping stations and the last for the city-owned fuel depot, and that'll be your first stop of the day after a prolonged coffee break. You deserve it. Afterall, you've been at work for an hour by now, sitting, awaiting the arrival of your Swampers. Today, you have Clyde and Brianne.

If they're not fucking, you're not trucking.

You drive a Class-3 International, so you're *pretty much* trucking.

Clyde and Brianne are *definitely* fucking. Look how wide Clyde smiles, his cheeks permanently red; Brianne's hair mousy, tousled.

Good for them, you think.

Or was that Ken?

Sometimes it's hard to decipher who's at the helm and who's mopping the poop deck.

SIX

Listen:

For Ken, it's not all about sex, despite its importance. Ken is the boy inside the man, the boy that will live perpetually through memory until no memories of you nor Ken remain. Ken craves attention when what you crave is a cold beer and your regular spot on the sofa; Ken wants to lick Carrie Underwood's legs; Ken wants to tell your Mother-In-Law to shut her fat cunt mouth and to stop gossiping about her mother and her sisters already because holy shit it's been the same thing for ten fuckin' years, man; Ken wants you to trade in your efficient 2009 Dodge Caliber, orange, for something with eight cylinders and a sound system that rumbles rib cages. Ken wants you to put down that bacon double cheeseburger and head to the gym not because exercise is good for you but because going to the gym and retiring such foods makes you look better to others. Hardly does anything Ken like have anything to do with yourself as much as how it makes you appear in the greater picture, which is fucking preposterous if you really think about it.

But Ken's a good guy, you know he means well. Remember: he's the *boy in you,* your lone connection to better—

No—

Simply put: Ken is your connection to days past. You have no complaints about your life. You have Boris, you have your wife, and you love them, and they love *you*.

They're everything.

But Ken…

Ken is everything else—

No.

You have what you need. You may not have needed that bacon double cheeseburger, but we all deserve a treat every now and again—including that heaped twinkling mound of grease-imbued Yukon gold potatoes that pair wonderfully with malt vinegar and gravy.

God, did they ever.

SEVEN

See:

Your house. It's nothing special, but then again neither are you. You and your house are a good match.

See:

Wifey on the couch with Boris on her breast, suckling.

Plump jugs.

Throb.

You say, "Hi, wife."

"Hello, husband," Wifey replies. Boris burps, vomits emotionlessly. Wifey hoists him up, lightly taps his back in aid of getting the burp out from his wee stomach deeps. Milk squirts in a thread-thin line from your wife's nipple onto the particle board coffee table.

Yikes!

You grab a lager from the fridge, you give you wife a careful kiss on the top of her head—mindful not to make a big deal of it because she's shared her distaste of being touched. You know her limits. You know a soft kiss where you kissed her is totally fine. It is. You head to take a shower.

"It's been six weeks," says your wife.

You tell your wife that you'll take your shower after you get *just a little dirtier,* and then you lecherously wink, and you open your beer and enjoy it on the couch to the tune of droll evening news—oh, how fucked up the world is, and oh what a surprise Boris is in for once he's of age to comprehend this disaster he's inherited.

Poor guy.

But at least the six weeks are up.

At least the three of you are together, and that, afterall, is the only world that matters.

EIGHT

The vagina is a remarkable object. Did you know that *Vagina,* is Latin for *Sheath?*

About your wife's *Sheath*:

It's as good as new! No signs of childbirth linger aside from the episiotomy scar which freaks you out at first—it looks a little like a tear-drop tattoo, sliced right from the vagina itself in a line that lilts to the left—but then you realize you're balls-deep and further on you hump, hump, hump because nothing else matters because you're balls-deep doggystyle and it's been six weeks. You're enjoying yourself, scrunching your face up with subsequent thrusts, grunting. Wifey seems to be enjoying herself, too, and sex is strong on the air.

Oh, how delightfully stinky—so pungent, a touch tangy, kinda like your ass crack.

Your romp in the sheets went like so:

Pump pump squirt.

But slowed down it went like this:

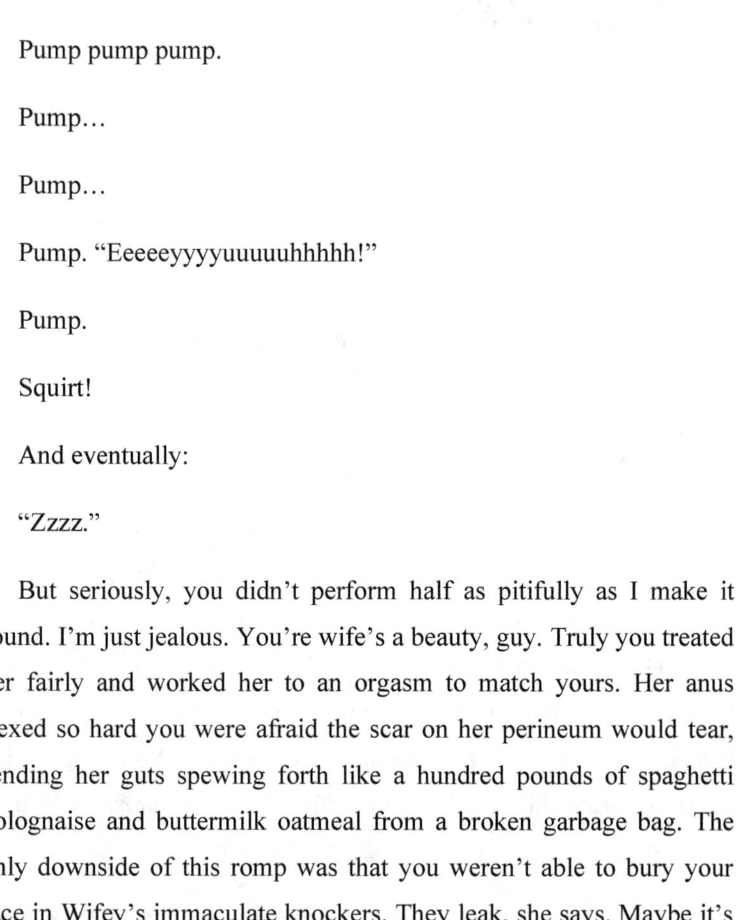

Pump…pump…

Pump pump pump.

Pump…

Pump…

Pump. “Eeeeeyyyyuuuuuhhhhh!”

Pump.

Squirt!

And eventually:

“Zzzz.”

But seriously, you didn’t perform half as pitifully as I make it sound. I’m just jealous. You’re wife’s a beauty, guy. Truly you treated her fairly and worked her to an orgasm to match yours. Her anus flexed so hard you were afraid the scar on her perineum would tear, sending her guts spewing forth like a hundred pounds of spaghetti bolognaise and buttermilk oatmeal from a broken garbage bag. The only downside of this romp was that you weren’t able to bury your face in Wifey’s immaculate knockers. They leak, she says. Maybe it’s for the better you *don’t* bury your face in her boobs so soon anyways.

Give it a couple weeks, you say—or so you dream. You see two wet spots on the mattress—this is where her milkers rested while you boinked her from the back. They leaked, like Wifey said they would.

Your wife rolls off the bed and heads into the ensuite for a shower. The water hisses, you tidy yourself up, re-establish order to the mussed sheets. You stand by the open window, let the cool spring breeze wash over your naked torso. You wave to your neighbour, Stuart, who's hosting a pool party for his ten-year-old daughter's soccer team. Stuart's smile suggests he knows what you were up to and he shoots you a thumbs-up and a knowing nod. Proud of yourself, you wink. Stuart's wife named Joan appears and she slaps his shoulder, shakes her head in your direction as though catching you in the fallout of a mortal sin—the fuckin' bitch. If Stuart made love to her like you made love to Wifey she'd understand the noise, your wife's cries of brilliant pleasure and all the contorted silhouettes. Wifey sounded like a banshee, you think, you dream. But who gives a shit?

No one.

You tell Ken to shut up.

Ken shuts up, but only after you exit your bedroom with your butt-cheeks waggling in heading for the mini bar to pour yourself a single-malt: Glenmorangie 15-Year. You lift a bottle of Jameson as a chaser and carry it with you to the bedroom, plus a couple extra glasses. You poke your head through the ensuite's door. You ask your wife if she wants a drink. She says she does. "Ice," she says. You get the ice, sit in bed, pour a drink, pour Wifey a drink. You take a drink on Boris's behalf whose bassinet has been placed just outside the bedroom door because he's much too young to experience the griminess of sexual intercourse. He sleeps soundly. Once your wife's out of the shower you hop in for yourself. You desperately need to cleanse yourself of the love which came in the form of a cast of briny sweat. The hot water is tantalizing on your flesh. You even wash your fuckin' hair!

It's 10:45 PM!

It's probably just the whisky.

Anyways, the shower's done. You dry yourself off and slide on your favourite pair of underwear—they're so old and flappy that you wear them with a belt. In the bed which you've re-dubbed as grounds upon which to regularly soil, Wifey gives Boris a late-night feed. She's bare naked.

Throb.

You sip your whisky to sober you up.

No luck.

Throb.

Throb.

Your wife sips her whisky.

Throb.

"Fuck," you say-but-don't-say, and you tuck yourself into the musky bed sheets as Stuart and Joan's pool-party persists to the sound of splish-splashes and plunks and gay laughter. Cheap pizza wafts into the bedroom upon the breeze and this smell blends inspiringly with the smell of ass crack and lingering semen. You don't know where the smell of semen is coming from so you're mildly perturbed—possibly further aroused—but you're sobered by the waft of baby powder and Boris's occasional coo. You feel guilty for committing what you did to Boris's mother, for tying her legs up behind her head and calling her a filthy whore, threatening to get the ball-gag and the cuffs and the flogger. You pinch Boris's toe, and then you lean over and give it a kiss. Your cheek inadvertently brushes your wife's nipple and she punches you in the shoulder. It hurts. You retreat further into your side of the bed, you wink.

Your wife gives you a look that says, Go fuck yourself. It's reassuring to know that the two of you are on the same page, but you don't forfeit hope—no, not yet. You take a whisky. You read your book.

Boris sleeps, your wife places him in his bassinet which is now bedside. He's so fragile there, so thin, so small.

Your wife's still naked, and to your delight she makes the first move. She delicately cups your balls like she's blindly inspecting a mandarin orange. She massages, and massages. Blah blah blah, you're hard. Sweet. Your dickhead peeks outta the fly of your baggy undershorts, a curious finch from an heirloom birdhouse.

This is what happens when sexual needs are mutually supressed for several weeks.

This is what happens after you're both reminded of that so-sweet taste of coitus:

You screw several times with the vigor of a caffeinated twelve-year-old boy. Boris sleeps through the second round—both you and your wife kept reasonably quiet—but come the third round, blended with a few ounces of Irish whiskey, out slips the occasional moan.

"Mmmmmmmm yeah!"

"Eeeeeyyyyuuuuuhhhhh!"

And Boris stirs, and Boris wakes while your nuts clap repeatedly against your wife's asshole like

CLAP CLAP CLAP CLAP CLAP.

Boris cries, your wife pleads that you keep going but that it's imperative you "Hurry up!" she says. "Mmmmmmm yeah!"

"Eeeeeyyyyuuuuuhhhhh!"

You turn it up a notch so that you're not pumping, you're not humping, you're not screwing. You're fucking.

You're *utterly,* inarguably *fucking.* There's no mistaking it.

Your headboard is banging against the wall and the box spring squeaks. Stuart and Joan surely think that *Stomp* is performing in the bedroom one yard over. Hopefully they can't hear Boris's wailing, you think. You still smell the pizza. Is that pepperoni?

Again, Wifey urges "Hurry up!"

"Eeeeeyyyyuuuuuhhhhh!"

Your wife's top-half is nearly in Boris's bassinet entirely. All you see are two jiggling hams and something yucky going into something yuckier and going in and out and in and out and in and out like the one yucky thing is really angry at the other yucky thing.

Splish splash.

You can't tell if that's the kids swimming next door or if it's of your own doing.

"Mmmmmmm yeah!"

"Eeeeeyyyyuuuuuhhhhh!"

"Hurry up, though!"

"Okay!" you say, and pump

And pump and pump and

"Eeeeeyyyyuuuuuhhhhh!"

And pump—

Squirt.

"Zzzz."

NINE

It's rare on weekends that you wear anything other than sweatpants with one of your two white tank-tops that are more yellow than white. Your wife is often found wearing black full-bum gotch and a t-shirt that makes her look like Grimace, the Hamburgler. She'll put pants on should there be any visitors. Leggings. Or if she goes grocery shopping. Or, for that matter, if she leaves the house at all. She no longer has the ass she had when she was in her early twenties. Oh, what an ass that ass was—'twas an ass to flaunt where and whenever possible.

Oh, what an ass…

You can find her on the couch, oftentimes holding Boris—the little guy's in a phase where he doesn't like being put down. The gyrating sitting-device proven to be so useful during Boris's early months gathers dust. You store your oranges there.

Since the sexual tension between you and your wife finally reached its popping-point the pair of you have resorted to a familiar schedule: once or twice a week, hardly ever on a Wednesday or following a particularly greasy dinner. You and your wife unconsciously smell the pheromones on Friday like clockwork, and these desires are obliged, often with added zest.

It's been a few weeks since that eventful night and the following morning where Stuart, your neighbour, came knocking—blushing—to drop off some leftover pizza. What a good guy, you thought, even though you were sure Joan sent him over to ensure you hadn't pummeled your wife to jelly.

The next person to knock on the door, though, is Ken.

That event goes like this:

"Have you ever thought about going on a vacation?" asks that plastic dink.

"Not since I was…twenty-one?" you surmise.

"Where did you go?"

You didn't go anywhere. You didn't have enough money and your credit card was maxed out. You also had only two friends:

Gyles and Kilgore.

You don't talk to them anymore because they moved cross-country in a pilgrimage to open a restaurant. Now they make a lot of money. You could've been making a lot of money too, but you fell in love instead.

Regrettably—

Or so at least you tell yourself whenever you're reminded of Gyles and Kilgore and your missed-out wealth. Common sense tells you that you're wealthier now than you could've been any other way, but Ken-the-cunt never hesitates to raise his objections.

"The money was there for you if you headed out with them," Ken reminds. "Coulda went out there, took that salary they offered you to chef the place and you coulda moved back with a few hundred grand in your pocket. And *then* you coulda got back together with the wife."

Coulda woulda shoulda.

Yeah, hindsight's 20/20—or whateverthefuck they say.

"Get outta here," you say to Ken, who occupies the non-existent void between you and your wife on the sofa. Your wife looks at you as though you're nuts. "Who are you talking to?" she asks.

You tell her that you're talking to no one—that you're tired and a little bummed that you're nearing the series finale of Breaking Bad, again, and you never want it to end; it always feels the same. What will occupy the television screen when there is no more? Mad Men, again?

Probably.

Ken's favourite show.

"Go visit your buddies," Ken says. "You know they'll have you back. They'll hire you in an instant, you know it."

You know Ken's right. Kilgore sent you a text congratulating you on the new son. **If you're open to moving out here**, the text read, **you know we've got a spot for you**.

But you know where your spot is, you think.

You're in it.

Yeah, you think.

You're in it, and you're happy. The sofa is moulded to the shape of your bony bottom.

You tell Ken, silently this time, to leave you be. He's having none of it.

"Stop lying to yourself."

"Fuck you!"

Your wife slaps you in the face.

"Sorry dear, wasn't talking to you."

Your wife rolls her eyes. "I *fucking* hate this show," she says. She's talking about Breaking Bad.

Aside from occupying the TV screen for several hundred days, what did Walter White ever do to her?

Anyways, morning passes and you enjoy a chicken salad sandwich for lunch. You dip it in Campbell's tomato soup—that always hits the spot. Ken lurks in the shadows through the morning, watching, looking for weak parts to poke through in hopes that it rears something ugly in you. You're running low on beer so you share with Wifey that you're going to the beer store. She asks you to pick her up a couple cans of something not-beer. You say that won't be a problem and you head out to fetch her a couple whisky & colas but no matter how fast nor the number of steps you log you cannot outrun Ken who says to you "I'm not going anywhere," and you walk faster and he's right on your tail and you speed up but he's still there and his grip is horribly strong.

TEN

There is minimal glamour in fatherhood—motherhood, too, while we're on the point. There's nothing clean about it unless you're filthy rich, and if that's the case, you pay the nanny to get dirty on your behalf. At times a grandmother will get dirty for you, but that usually comes with its fair share of consequent messes, such as misplaced dishes, misplaced cutlery, passive aggression, reminders that *"When you were a baby I* loved *being a stay-at-home parent—it was wonderful. I* loved *it,"* and reminders that, though totally ignorant, life was incomparably affordable in the 80s and 90s, and that *It's not that hard these days, is it?* What's critical here is to withhold the "Fuck off, bitch," because grandmas give good Christmas gifts.

A lot of people use their babies as accessories.

Don't be this kind of person.

If you are this kind of person:

You're a cunt.

But, on glamour:

There is a Mom-Blogger on the internet whose online handle is something like *thetotallyidealbutunattainablemotherhoodexperiece.*

Your wife's her biggest fan.

This Mom-Blogger's Instagram is hewn together with the precision of a Japanese tattooist and lean as though all it consumes is chicken and spinach washed down with water and Ex-Lax. The pastels are trim and bright and the lines are strong and the photographs are edited to perfection so much so that you can't spot a single blemish. This Mom-Blogger's husband is an award-winning musician and an architect in his spare time. The Mom-Blogger consults as an interior design specialist, and together, their home is worth upwards of $15,000,000. The Mom-Blogger is considered an influencer to boot, and her page is laden with sponsored posts for products that no bourgeois asshole could afford.

You fucking hate this bitch. In your spare time you brainstorm the various ways you could get away with cutting off her head. You'd hang it from your door with cast-iron ring speared through its ears as a doorknocker and long for her children to come Trick or Treating. Fuck her kids, too. You know for a fact they're going to become entitled wankers, gifted prosperous futures and likely to play hockey or American Football—some sport where they could get away with violence less than shooting up a preparatory school—

But your wife loves this woman and defends her against your wry musings.

"Dear, that stroller is probably worth more than our orange Dodge Caliber," you say.

"Yeah, probably," Wifey goes. "It's still nice, though."

See, with comments like the former all you're doing is trying to manage your wife's expectations—to knock her down a rung, to a sober level so she doesn't get down on herself when realizing that your middle-class household income accosts *barely* enough to get through month-to-month. She'll act unbothered while watching this woman proceed through her idyllic life with the help of filters, and whether she's aware of it, she's lying. Your wife wants this life, and she doesn't care about your opinion.

Oftentimes, this is when you prepare for an argument.

Or drunk sex.

But probably just an argument.

"Oh, see. Not bad," your wife says a moment later. "It costs only nine-thousand dollars."

"What is?" you ask. You hope she's talking about that charcoal barbecue you told her about a few weeks ago. You really got to replace your decade-old Broil King.

She shows you a picture of the stroller. This thing comes about as ugly as they get, something you could find at one of the town's Thrift Shops for less than fifty bucks with its wiry frame and plump cushions and copper gildings.

You say, "Should I start sucking dick or should you?"

"Oh, fuck off," says Wifey.

"Should Boris? We could probably pimp him out for twenty-times the amount we'd get for ourselves. He doesn't even have any teeth yet. Gummy blowjobs are *great.*"

Your wife punches your shoulder, says "Just let me dream a little bit," and then resumes scrolling. You've watched her scope these same photos a hundred times before. You say nothing else because you acknowledge the importance of having dreams. You dream of a barbecue the size of a garden shed, only not *quite* as big. The barbecue you dream of could go as a sideways refrigerator, and you'd cook a lot of good stuff in there.

Embrace the inadequacy, bucko.

Ken tells you to take the job with Gyles and Kilgore.

You tell Ken to shut up.

Ken shuts up.

But you can't help the tantalizing thoughts knocking and knocking around in your head, teasing you with the possibility of *more*. These thoughts are there and these thoughts are yours to cope with. You have yet to tell Wifey that Gyles and Kilgore got back in touch. You doubt you ever will. Boris doesn't need a $9000 stroller. Boris doesn't need three-quarters of the shit he already has.

HE DOESN'T EVEN KNOW HE *HAS* THE SHIT HE HAS!

That afternoon you and your family go to the zoo. Boris can hardly see two feet from the end of his nose, he still thinks he's just in a really big womb. When people talk to him, commenting on his funny little hat, his eyes dart back and forth in search of whatever's doing the talking. He never finds what he's looking for and *definitely* doesn't know who *Darling* is, or who *Precious* or *Handsome* or *Studmuffin* is. Becoming a father has really made you dislike other people. *Fuck* other people, especially that Instragram broad who your wife so obviously looks up to. And fuck her husband. Fuck her kids. Again.

The zoo's cafeteria is about as comfortable to eat in as it is to let a colony of bees build their hive in your rectum. This hurts. Eating a discouraging $45 lunch in a zoo cafeteria isn't *painful,* per se, but the cafeteria smells like socks and canola oil and the floors of a dozen Toyota Siennas. It *might* smell a touch like vomit, because the yellow stains of that fat kid's souvenir t-shirt are suspect at best. There is a pack of wolves on the fat kid's t-shirt, and the t-shirt is the colour of a winter's dusken sky. The fat kid is *so* fat, and he's wearing grey sweatpants. He wipes his fucking nose with the palm of his hand and then inspects the product.

This is where you experience your first suicidal thought.

I should kill myself, you think.

The only problem is that you don't have a gun because the only reason to have a gun is to shoot it and you have nothing to shoot, so, you don't have a gun.

Can I kill myself with off-brand ibuprofen?

If you *really* want to, sure.

You know where the lion paddock is, though. That would be easier. It's probable that they'd go for the throat.

I do want to kill myself, you think. *I do know where the lion paddock is, too.* You prepare to stand, hands flat on the table—

"Hello."

You look to your right.

The fat kid stands there.

"My name's Thomas."

You look to your wife in hopes that she'll tell you what to do.

Thomas goes, "Tee. Aitch. Oh. Em. Eh. Ess."

You look at this kid like he's a talking loaf of bread. "What?" you ask.

"Tee. Aitch. Oh. Em. Eh. Ess."

This kid smells like shoes.

You look at your wife. You don't know why you're looking at your wife.

"My name's Thomas."

"Hi," says you.

"Tee. Aitch. Oh. Em. Eh. Ess."

The Alpha wolf howls at a blood moon and the remainder of his pack bay in reprise. They're in a forest of evergreens, perched atop a rockface with various shrubbery sprouting from the sides. You notice a magnificent bald eagle soaring through the sky. You think of The United States of America while looking at this bald eagle and the chunky not-so-little-little-boy, vomit on his tight tee, snot leaking from his snout, boogers crusted all over its nostrils like stalactites.

This encompasses the United States, you think:

Fat kids and eagles.

You don't know why you say it, but you ask Tee Aitch Oh Em Eh Ess "Are you having a good day?" like you actually care about him.

Tee Aitch Oh Em Eh Ess says, "My name's Thomas."

And then he sneezes in your face.

Yes, that smell you noted earlier *was* vomit, and you can taste Thomas's breakfast.

Buttery scrambled eggs. Sausage. More sausage. More Sausage. More sausage. And he hasn't brushed his teeth. You can taste last night's supper:

Hot dogs. Lots of ketchup. Freezer-burned fries. Sausage.

When the mist settles, you see red. *All* you see is red, as a matter of fact.

This is because Thomas's mom appeared.

She's as big as a fucking house! She's wearing red leggings that leave nothing to the imagination.

Yes, her ass looks like it has been beaten with a burlap sack filled with dimes. Her ass has been rendered to the consistency of a bowl of wet popcorn. Her buttocks flap like a turkey's wattle.

You should've killed yourself when you had the chance because you wake up the next morning with a cold and you're too sick to get out of bed to hang yourself.

You have nightmares about this piggie and his grey sweatpants yet you dream about punching him square in the nose and watching him cry

Wee wee wee wee

All the way home.

That was Boris's first trip to the zoo.

ELEVEN

This is your first Cold as a father and it's worse than you imagined. You knew it would be bad, but you simply could not fathom how torturous it would be when your entire household has come down with matching symptoms. Boris cries through the day; everybody's sniffling; everybody's grouped on the sofa and you've familiarized yourself thoroughly with The Wiggles, Sesame Street, Bluey, Blue's Clues, and the fact that for the TV to hold Boris's attention the volume must be set to an ungodly level and not a sniff lower than gobsmackingly loud.

You're miserable; you're sweaty; today you've already taken three baths and have had your daily fill of Tylenol. Your asthma is bad; you've had five cans of Campbell's Chicken Soup loaded with garlic and black pepper and turmeric. Naturopaths can go fuck themselves—none of this bullshit works. You still feel like garbage. You make a hot toddy. You make five hot toddies; you drink them all. You feel worse.

Now it's important to note that the common cold is unavoidable. Every child but your own is a fucking germ. Every child but your own is a Tee Aitch Oh Em Eh Ess. Colds are an initiation through parenthood and childhood. Acclimate yourself with this feeling. This feeling is *you.* This feeling is infancy-through-middle-school.

Acclimate yourself with force-feeding Boris medicine. Look for alternatives if he dumbly lets it slide out his mouth, which is likely what will happen. Prepare yourself for the cries.

Boris is crying.

Wifey tried giving him some Motrin.

It's leaking out the corner of his wailing maw. Boris sounds like Private Torres from Day of the Dead when the zombies are ripping off his head and stretching his vocal cords like they're making fresh pasta. You find yourself staring out the window because these cries numb you; they turn you into a vegetable. You're Stephen Hawking but a long from being a genius.

Wifey asks for help.

You stand up with your hair all fucked around and greasy. "What do you want me to do?" you ask.

"Hold his fucking hands down Jesus!"

"What does Jesus have to do with this?"

Your wife, reasonably, ignores your smart-alecky remark.

Boris is looking at you as though asking for help. You can imagine his voice:

Help me daddy, help me daddy! I don't want da medicine! It's so yucky!

Wifey attempts giving him another dose but his small hand knocks the syringe and she misfires, shoots it onto the couch and then goes on to bitch about now needing to take a towel to the upholstery.

"Just hold his hands!" says Wifey. "This will help his fever."

Very loud cries.

Flailing arms, which you grab. You hold them. That's all you do. You don't apply any force whatsoever aside from holding them and your efforts are enough to nullify any of Boris's attempts at wriggling free. You've immobilized him—you're a savage beast.

Wifey pinches Boris chin, his mouth opens. She slowly plunges the syringe of Motrin into his mouth.

It goes down, mostly. Some leaked out, but not much.

You release Boris's hands and hoist him up, rubbing his back. You tell him you love him and that he's tough and that he's tougher than you've ever been and that you love him. You love Boris and you're sorry.

"I love you, son," you say.

Boris just cries because he doesn't know how to talk. Also, he was just restrained as though he were a patient in a mental asylum. You feel like you could do with a cry; you feel for the little guy. Your wife has headed into the kitchen to return the medicine to its spot on the shelf.

"Want some tea?" she asks.

"TEA?!" you bark. "You're offering me tea after we've just tortured our offspring?!"

Your wife rolls her eyes. She puts enough water in the kettle for the both of you, puts a couple teabags in a couple cups and then returns to her spot on the sofa, heaves out a withering bosom.

"Time for some lunch," she says.

Throb.

"Eeeeeyyyyuuuuuhhhhh!"

"Bless you," says Wifey.

You say "Thanks" and hand her your son.

He feasts.

He sleeps.

So do you.

TWELVE

In your dreams Tee Aitch Oh Em Eh Ess stands oafishly there.

Or is this a nightmare?

Lions growl in the foreground softly and a noose hangs beside the vending machines next to the shitters and you're unable to go to it because you're bound to the table in casts of mitten-like booger heaps.

Wet popcorn.

Certainly, this is a nightmare.

You're in a mist of sodium-riddled discharge and Tee Aitch Oh Em Eh Ess approaches without moving a muscle. He hovers towards you; you're stuck at the table.

"My name's Thomas," he says, his voice snug in your ears next to your eardrums though there's a distance to it—reverb, in an auditory sense; you're in one corner of an Olympic gymnasium and he's in the one furthest away, unimpeded. The wolves upon his t-shirt nuzzle into one another and stars shoot across the night sky and the alpha male howls. Thomas's t-shirt is a television; the elements to his souvenir tee are alive and frolicking through a night wood like a good screensaver. The wolf howls again.

You understand the howling wolf.

It says:

"Suppertime!"

Another wolf drags an elk carcass out from the trees, and so on.

"Tee Aitch Oh Em Eh Ess."

"Yeah, fuckin' *Thomas;* I get it," you say.

Thomas morphs into a wolf and he leaps atop you and his paws are lead bricks on your chest and drool hangs from his mouth in a thumb-sized thread, a spaghetti noodle. And then it's all gone—yes—because as it is in dreams you find yourself in one place and then suddenly in another without an explanation behind how it happened. You are in the Setting on Thomas's t-shirt, and dozens of disembodied wolf-eyes hover inside the pitch-black verge.

"Be *better,*" Thomas barks, and slowly these barks spread through the rest of his pack. Soon the night is filled with a choir of barks pleading for you to *Be Better* and it's at this point where you realize that you're dreaming, and you feel reality tugging at you as though there are two meat hooks latched to your orbital bones and tugging. As you're forcefully removed from your dream you hear your cell phone's text message notification, and then you hear the sound of a ribeye steak striking a butter-filled cast iron pan. You smell rosemary and nuttiness.

You're waking up.

This isn't necessarily a bad thing.

But what is it that you have to be better towards? You don't think you've been all that bad—

You *haven't* been all that bad. You're happy; your wife's happy; Boris is happy— probably…at least you'd like to think that.

Before you can ask the question you're looking at your bedroom ceiling and your nose feels like it's full of sand; beneath a cake of snot. You feel the mucus at the base of your throat and it's pooled there and you cough

Cough

Cough.

You cough until you're sitting up, and you cough some more until you muster the strength to stand. You grab your sweats, a toque, the baggiest hoodie you have, your cell phone, and head into the bathroom where you blow your nose so hard you tear the Kleenex and snot into your palm. There's a lot. It's green with white lines through it.

Yuck.

You cell phone chimes.

It's Kilgore.

The offer is an annual $125,000—moving expenses included—and the Chef Jacket.

THIRTEEN

Such a salary is double what you make already and in accepting the gig you'd have ability to do what you love professionally—an opportunity not many people *at all* are blessed with. You've long considered this a Heaven on earth, the chance to run your own kitchen at a hearty salary *while* being a father to your son and a husband to your wife—your wife, in particular.

That's it.

That's all.

Nothing special—

Nothing special at all.

These are just your dreams and currently they invite you in with open arms and dinner's ready on the table and dinner's lookin' fuckin' good.

In the mirror, you don't see yourself. Ken returns your gaze and he grins fiendishly; he tells you that you'll be the one in charge of your schedule; that you can fly back at least twice a month with cash to spare living so upper-classedly.

You tell Ken that you wouldn't move out there on your own.

Ken says that in due course Wifey and Boris can come out and join you there; that they'll be plenty of room in the new house—he seems so sure of it. "Give it a few months," Ken says. "It'll take a while to find a new place, but one will come up and it'll be better than *this* dump."

Sternly you tell him "No." You're proud of your meager home, and you get to brushing your teeth. You wash your hands, you wash your face. You head downstairs, make some coffee. It's 6:45 AM.

You watch the world go for what seems like hours until Wifey comes downstairs with Boris in hand.

"Good morning," you say.

You kiss them.

You sit down to watch the world go by as you do *this* and only this….

That's all there is to do and you tell yourself you're okay with that.

FOURTEEN

Ten days pass before your cold subsides whereas Boris and Wifey got over theirs within the week. Your bitching is getting ridiculous already and all you want is a little bit of peace and quiet as free now from the common cold Boris has suddenly taken a liking to crawling and all he does is fucking fail; he gets to his hands and knees and faceplants, bloodies his precious little nose and cries louder, but tries again.

He's made minimal progress over the last while, but progress is progress; when he gets going it looks like he's making sweet, sweet love to the rug, and then he tips over in a pile of tears—just like he's made sweet, sweet love to the rug. This is the circle of becoming a functionable human.

You told your wife about Gyles and Kilgore's offer.

She said no, and you can't blame her.

This is why:

You used to boink her in dry storage; you used to plonk her in the walk-in; you fucked her in the men's bathroom, the women's bathroom, and the guest bathrooms—even the handicap washroom! Wifey once went through an entire dinner service with myoglobin stains on her blouse and handprints around her waist!

Before your wife, there were others—a whole waitstaff of them.

Working in restaurants, especially with Gyles and Kilgore, would be the end of everything. You know this. The temptation for tomfoolery is too much, you acknowledge this, and you have your message typed and ready for sending in a three-way chat with your two old buddies.

You guys know I love you both, the would-be text message reads, **and I thank you both for the opportunity, but I can't up uproot my family**.

That's it. One text and you can be done with all this lo you feign from sending it because your dreams are *so* close and you're due at work in two hours and you fucking *loathe* the mere idea of that place—it may as well be tuberculosis. You hate the fake shit you find there, the nonsmiles behind all the smiles, the nonhappy behind all the happy. For twice your current salary you can love going to work and do something with your life; you'd make enough to leave Boris a little something after you die; you'd make enough to go on a couple vacations each year—vacations that went to places grander than your grandparents' old log cabin.

But that's not the way love works.

You tell Gyles and Kilgore that you'll let them know within the week.

They're okay with this.

Now:

Lunch at your Mother-in-Law's.

Sorry about that.

All the windows are closed and it's 79° in there and your wife's darling mom is cold despite the geriatric grey-haired black lab on her lap, the border collie sitting across her slippered feet, and the bullmastiff draped around her fucking shoulders.

Dog hair lay clumped in corners and you wouldn't investigate beneath the sofas for one-million dollars cash because surely the dust bunnies spawn and breed down there among the diseases developing in the crannies and nooks of your in-laws' festering abode. There's a piano no one knows how to play, a 70-inch television that plays strictly the news—you have no option to watch anything else because they only have basic cable and even if they had your favourites available for watching you'd never consider watching Breaking Bad or Mad Men here, no one would get it, and watching a good show with bad company usually means not enjoying your show. Furniture is laden with dog hair; everything is dusty—inexplicably dusty—and this house smells like the inside of a vacuum bag.

You think, *fuck this place,* as you munch your fourth Benadryl of the afternoon, cooped up in the washroom and rubbing your face with cold water. You've been there for ten minutes; the allergy meds have you feeling a little bit giggly but quite tuckered.

Boris often wails because everything is *so* goddamn loud. Luckily your ears are plugged due to the constant nose-blowing, yet your wife and mother-in-law talk, and talk, and talk, and repeat what they were just talking about, and talk, and then pause for a second, and then pick-up where they left off—the first topic of the day: the stupidity of some stupid cooze from work who wears too much perfume and hosts quarterly Pampered Chef parties. Your wife and mother are scheduled to go to one despite their obvious distaste towards this smelly woman whose name is obviously Barbara.

You feel like Boris.

Your father-in-law, who's a good man, gets it. He asks if you'd like to go outside.

You do.

You bring four beers for the two of you and bullshit the afternoon away as the three large dogs rampage through the backyard, drooling, crapping, barking at the neighbour who's just trying to plant some fucking strawberries, man. They don't appear too pleased—the neighbour. Your father-in-law doesn't seem to care.

Whatever—to draw breath is to give Wifey an orgasm strictly by penetration.

"Don't tell my wife," you say. "Your daughter, I mean," your clarify. "But I got offered a gig at my buddies' restaurant. Six figures," you say.

"Whereabouts?" Daryl inquires.

You tell him that it's located far away, and then you watch him wince. "Are you going to take it?" he asks. Obviously, this is a quiz. You expected this.

"No," you say.

Daryl's halfway through his beer already. "You don't want to be moving so far away with a newborn anyways," he says. "You're valued as a cook by your family. You were a hell of a line-cook back in the day, guy."

You say thanks.

Your father-in-law says you're welcome, or something like that—your ears are still plugged, and seemingly worsening. Your eyes are made of paper mâché—it's easy to miss out on the fine details of things when they're in this inflamed state.

Two beers through, you head inside for more. Daryl's got a full twenty-four at the ready as he knows you're a heavy drinker, socially, and he's such a guy, too. He ignites the barbecue, throws on a dozen hot dogs on there because your mother-in-law is of the ilk who doesn't recognize the value of a good bratwurst. Afterall, she's not the one who's forced to deal with your putrid flatulence.

Your father-in-law's grill matches the worth of your 2009 Dodge Caliber.

Your 2009 Dodge Caliber is orange.

Feeling loose, and even though what's cooking are hot dogs, you say to your father-in-law, "Sit! I'll man the grill! I'll get it all outta me," you say—feeling your three beers mingling curiously with all that Benadryl. You grazed for breakfast, too— nuts, mostly. You want to feel like the Head Chef of a restaurant with an a la carte menu.

You dice white onion despite your in-laws' blunt Cutco knives. "We need sauerkraut!" you say, and you get it from the fridge, put a few spoonfuls into a glass ramekin; you taste it, you add a pinch of salt and a half-pinch of pepper. You close the grill's lid until the wieners whistle. You butter the buns, toast them, stack the perfect hot dogs on a platter and stack the buns on another.

Lunch time—

No, wait.

Pee time.

Ken's waiting for you in the mirror and he's smiling as wide as you've seen him smile in upwards of eighteen months.

Ken says hi.

Hi.

Ken notes that you feel good. Ken notes that he's happy for you.

You *do* feel good—despite your allergies, your tight chest. You thank Ken for feeling happy for you—you're happy that somebody's happy for you.

Without thinking it, you grab your phone. You sit on the crapper with your pants on—you don't have to shit; you just feel good, and doing a bit of scrolling will only add a few endorphins to your restrained operating system. You find nothing on social media but in your messaging app your text stands at the ready in the group chat with Gyles and Kilgore and you delete it, replace the words.

You send:

Book me a ticket bros. I'll come out for a weekend to check the place out.

By the time you get home, you receive the reply:

Three weeks from now?

You reply,

Deal.

Suddenly you no longer feel the twelve beers you drank over lunch; you are nun-sober and struck with a longing for home even though you've yet to leave.

The homesickness settles in already.

FIFTEEN

Fuckhead, I need you to dwell on what you've done behind your wife's back. I'd like to know how you're going to tell her.

Are you going to tell her at all?

"No," you say.

That's what I thought.

How do you plan on going about this?

"Day by day."

Right.

You're hungover and your bowels, watery, expel ghosts of last night. Luckily your days of praying to the Porcelain Gods are through, you just give yourself a headache not unlike a migraine and no amount of sleep gets rid of it until the last sleep of the day. Your diet is limited to strictly broth and bananas and eggs.

A hangover cure you don't know about:

Three boullion packets mixed into a Gatorade of your choosing.

Electrolytes for the dehydration; sodium for water retention. Eat a couple fried eggs, yolk cooked through, and a couple pieces of dry toast to keep your stomach held together and you'll survive the day—you won't *feel* good, mind you, but this will help. Trust me.

See, it's challenging to be hungover and a dad simultaneously, kind of like how it is when you're sick, this time around the only exception being that nobody gives a fuck that you're hungover. You did this to yourself, Fuckhead, so buckle up, feed yourself a handful of Advil and help out; your wife's waiting. It's already nine-thirty in the morning and you've went from the bathroom to the bed five times since 4:00 AM.

Roll out of bed, feel the room spin, massage your scalp and watch the dandruff fall like snow to your black boxer shorts. Taste the alcohol which has burned its flavour into your esophagus, your tongue; dream of Listerine and chewing a pack of Excel Winter Mint but realize that these are only dreams, for you're stuck with this awful taste until noon and your belly will rumble with each sip of water.

Wifey's made coffee, and she says "Made you breakfast" while hovering over a mountain of bacon stacked atop a heap of scrambled eggs. She made hashbrowns, too—homemade, with sliced onions and garlic chunks. She doesn't understand hangovers, especially at this age, upon the cusp of your thirties. Your wife hasn't had a hangover since she was eighteen. She hardly drinks.

The smell of the buttery eggs disagrees with everything about you.

And your wife smiles, notes that your hair's all messed up. "Eat and then go take a shower," she says. "Or a bath." She gives you a kiss. "Your breath stinks," she says. You apologize. She reminds you to brush your tongue. "Right," you say, pulling out your seat at the table across from Boris who looks at you with wide eyes. You tell him you love him, and bid him good morning.

He says nothing because he doesn't have a good grasp on speaking just yet. It'll be a couple years yet. His eyes are big, though, and he enjoys splashing around in his applesauce. He licks his fingers.

A waft of egg steam goes up your nostrils and you gag and Wifey slides you a cup of coffee. You ask for a Tylenol; she gives you two Advil because Tylenol taken with alcohol in the system means liver failure. You wash down the Advil with your coffee and you gag again.

Your stomach rumbles disconcertedly, and you apologize in advance.

I understand, your stomach replies. Feel the alcohol-instilled guilt course through you. What did you stomach ever do to you to deserve such unfair treatment? *My poor body,* you think.

My body, my choice, you think.

You made the wrong choice.

Eggs and bacon and hashbrowns and garlic chunks doused in ketchup and garnished with salt and pepper. You take your first bite. Wifey threw together a wonderful plate, it's a shame you can't enjoy it to its full extent, to give this breakfast what it deserves: honour. It's a shame you haven't given your wife what *she* deserves:

Respect.

You went behind her back and told your buddies to book you a plane ticket out of town, and that ticket has been booked. Currently it sits pinned to the top of your Gmail Inbox, and Wifey knows nothing about it—

Tuck it away, truck through a chunk of this breakfast and dream of nighttime where you'll wake *tomorrow* and feel as good as new—go ahead, man, wish the day away. You'll sleep like a baby, tonight, so long as you make it.

There is plenty of throbbing afoot but none of it comes from tantalizing origins; whatever's in your stomach: it stirs, brews an insidious something; the kitchen spins and though what you eat is good for you, your body disagrees. You make it through half the plate and tell your wife you'll finish it later.

She doesn't mind.

It's now when Boris takes a poo. It sounds like somebody is blowing a raspberry into a Tupperware container when that container is buried beneath a dozen throw pillows and a large comforter. This sound is a strange sound.

"You got that one," says Wifey encouragingly.

SIXTEEN

You made it.

Good job.

You achieved normality comes day's end, more or less. You were able to stomach your leftover breakfast, you had a sandwich for supper—you were even able to take Boris out in his stroller for a half-hour while Wifey escaped for a bath and a half-hour with the lastest Stephen King. Despite your hangover you feel accomplished. The fresh air worked wonders.

Now you lay supine in bed, arm behind your pillow, accepting your mistake:

You should've stopped after the second hot dog.

These are lessons to take with you into tomorrow and beyond.

You shut your eyes. You Sleep.

"Hello."

It's Tee Aitch Oh Em Eh Ess—he was waiting for you there.

"Hi, Thomas," you say.

"My name's Thomas," says Thomas.

God, what an abortion.

Still the wolves on his tee howl and still yellow mustard stains the bottom; still, Thomas wears grey sweatpants and still he smells like shoes.

"How are you, Thomas?" you ask.

"I'm well, thank-you." Thomas's voice remains echo-like, ethereal, ghostly. He stands at your bedside, says further: "I'd like to show you your life should you accept the position at your friends' restaurant."

"Okay, Thomas," you reply— more or less some way along those lines.

Suddenly you're immobilized. You're unable to draw breath. There's something tight wrapped around your throat.

You can't move your hands—remember: you're *immobilized,* and if you don't understand that word I'm not sure how you've made it this far into a book.

The truth of the situation is actually that you're dead. This is evident when your lifeless body revolves until you see yourself reflected in a wall-length mirror. You've hanged yourself. You're swollen, bloated, the colour of a plum.

Yuck.

Finding your next breath is matched with orgasmic relief. You and Tee Aitch Oh Em Eh Ess are standing in nothing in particular. You're in wherever you go when you die, which is impossible to explain to a mortal so what you see is nothing. You're not cold, you're not hot, you're not warm. You simply *are.*

You like it here.

"So," you begin, thinking of the noose; thinking of the family you left behind for something a little bit more than middleclass. "I'll kill myself," you say.

Thomas nods.

You ask, "Was it worth it?"

Thomas lifts one of his sausagey digits, points. There's a door there. You start towards it, feet trodding over fog-covered earth—this is a foggy place. There are no bounds here, you might as well be in the heart of a field on a horrifying Hallowe'en night. All you hear are your footsteps meeting ground, the ground muffling them as best it can because nothing *alive* is supposed to be here.

Towards the door you stroll, Thomas leading the way with his wolf t-shirt ridden up his back to expose a fish-belly white torso. He has a mole the size of a fingernail crowning his ass crack and his waistband has left an imprint around his hips that looks like a Tonka truck had driven there.

On the air comes an angelic sound, a song. A choir. It sounds like they're singing in Italian—at least something fancier than mere English. The Italians invented pizza and Martin Scorsese. He makes wonderful movies.

When you push through the door you're greeted with a beam of light. You are in a sunlit room and the floor is hardwood and your feet are tacky upon it, clicking with each step because underfoot your feet are sweaty. Thomas burps. Here, in the ether of the beyond, you're still disgusted by this kid. The nastiness of gross children persists into the afterlife.

This is a fact.

And then a spry Mulatto girl enters the room, says "Come on, Boris! In here!" This young'un seems *so* happy.

A girlfriend at such a youthful age? Surely not.

Surely not.

Right?

No—

Wrong—

No—

Right—

No. You'll see.

Boris enters the room, slams the door but pays mind to what noise it makes as he shuts it. Your son is grown—at least ten, you figure. His hair is just like yours was when *you* were a boy; he stands around four feet tall, fifty pounds or thereabouts. A handsome lad, or so *you* think.

Thomas scratches his underbelly in the corner of the room.

The pair of you go unseen by these two youth.

Boris says, "We're in the clear," and sits on the bed on the room's opposite end and the Mulatto girl joins him once grabbing a book from the bookshelf:

How the Grinch Stole Christmas.

The girl reads.

Boris listens.

The girl rises to get another book:

Green Eggs and Ham.

Boris reads.

The girl listens, says, "Your turn."

Boris takes the two books and places them back on the shelf. He returns with *The Hobbit.*

The girl's hazel eyes are wide.

Boris reads the magical first line:

"*In a hole in the ground there lived a Hobbit.*"

And so on.

You were never much of a reader and you're stunned that your son reads—it's like you're listening to an audiobook. Boris doesn't falter; he reads the entirety of the first chapter and puts a bookmark at his spot and goes on to say that he'll read the second chapter after supper. The girl beams with excitement. "Let's go play outside," she says.

And they leave the room.

You and Thomas follow.

The house is a shocking upgrade from your current—or *former*—abode. The only rug in sight is an area rug beneath a coffee table with a surface as thick as a bank vault's wall. The furniture is vastly different from that Swedish shit, possibly from fucking *Restoration Hardware* considering the fact it looks like it may have been lost at sea for a couple decades, but it's *very* nice. There are photographs on the walls and you're not in any of them because you've killed yourself—you're long gone, man.

Boris and the girl play in the backyard, which is large. The grass is like the fairway at Augusta National and there's a swing set at the far end of the yard. The patio is of slate cobbles and a firepit sits in the middle surrounded by a matching set of chairs. The barbecue is one you're familiar with. It costs north of nine-thousand dollars—the size of a garden shed.

The vegetable garden—something Wifey's dreamt of for as long as you've known her—teems with verdancy. The flower garden is richer than a coke-peddling leprechaun who lives at the far-end of an immaculate double rainbow.

And so on.

What matters here is that Boris is happy.

You don't really care about this Mulatto girl because she doesn't come from you.

But where *did* she come from?

Thomas shows you.

Your wife's feet are pinned behind her head as she's being ran-through by a man with a cock twice the size of your own.

Throb—

But let's go back—

Back to the foreplay.

What's foreplay, you ask?

Well, to someone like you—someone who prefers to get right to the fuckin'—foreplay is a little bit of this a little bit of that before you get to the meat and potatoes of bedstuffery.

This is where the foreplay begins:

What surrounds you transitions into a cacophonous fruit-punch of colour and time. It's like you're in the Millennium Falcon at hyperdrive, only you're going backwards, through time and into the past.

A widow peruses a selection of fresh tomatoes at a Farmers' Market. This Widow is your wife—obviously. She's wearing a sundress—

Throb—

With Jesus-sandals on her feet.

Throb.

She has a floppy hat on her head.

....

And her bum is significant.

Throb.

Long story short, the proprietor of this stall has a hobby farm and he's got a couple miniature horses there, a couple cows, a couple of acres of farmland and a whole lotta patience. He also has goats and he's a dog person.

....

They talk a bit; he helps her select a few tomatoes and asks her if she'd wait around until the market closes so he could buy her a cup of coffee.

"Sure," the widow replies. She then goes on to say that her son is with her grandmother.

"Your partner won't mind?" the farmer asks.

"He committed suicide," the widow says matter-of-factly. "He took a job a few thousand miles away, cheated on me and took a bunch of pills one night because he hated his life and then he hanged himself."

The farmer says, "That's wonderful," and the widow smiles, says, "It is, isn't it," and beams further.

She's blushing.

And they get coffee,

And they exchange phone numbers and are texting one another regularly by the end of the night. A second date's been set:

Dinner and a movie.

Classic.

You're pulled forward through many dates, following the widow as she goes about her days with your son who'll never know his father—he was still young when this all began, no older than two. The widow follows a predicable routine:

She wakes up, feeds herself. She gets Boris, feeds Boris, drops Boris off at his grandmother's. She goes to work. She feeds herself. She gets Boris and then cooks supper for the both of them. She sleeps Boris. She sleeps herself. This repeats five days a week and it's proven through their many interactions that whenever the widow can afford to have someone watch her son, she's with the farmer. The farmer's growing on her, and you see in her a familiar smile that you once loved—

A smile you still love—

But a smile that, if this path is taken, you'll never see again.

You watch their first kiss, and now they hold hands. The widow has told your mother and her own that she's seeing someone new and they reply to this news with excitement, citing that she deserves this, and that Boris will be glad to have someone new around on occasion, but also warning her to be mindful; to check her calculations before things get too serious. The widow agrees.

What's over yon is predictable when the widow asks Boris's grandmother if she'll spend the night at the house. Boris's grandmother replies with a wry smile, "Sure," and says nothing further.

That night the widow goes directly to the farmer's house where he has put together a charcuterie board fit with brie cheese and raisins and chocolate and blueberries and candied nuts; he's readied a chateaubriand on a handcrafted board with perfectly grill-marked mushroom caps and rosemary sprigs to garnish. For sides he's roasted baby potatoes and broccoli and asparagus to dip in a homemade bearnaise.

You can practically feel the *widow* throbbing.

The farmer makes banana's foster for dessert.

And then it all begins with a blowjob.

Throb.

And the farmer goes down on the widow like there's fine whisky down there.

Throb.

And then they fuck.

Throb.

But the farmer's wearing a condom! A Trojan Magnum.

It catches the farmer's seed.

Eventually, they fall in love.

What else is there that you need to know?

You watch the dates; you watch them smile and you watch the farmer introduce himself to Boris, who, after a couple tear-filled meetings, now greets the farmer with smiles and lets him hold him. Boris is acclimated. He's forgotten about you.

You're dead. The farmer's alive—

Better men than you endure through the bullshit and have a thing for avoiding frivolity.

With love comes cravings deeper than mere boinking and taking another's hand in marriage.

I'll spare you, Fuckhead, from description exceeding that which I've already described; your wife's feet are pinned behind her head as she's run-through by the farmer, and you watch the farmer's taint pulse in harmony with the widow's, filling her with what will, in a few hours, be the beginnings of Boris's sister.

It went like this:

Pump pump

Squirt.

SEVENTEEN

You're expendable so long as you're not the best you can be,

So,

At the very least,

For fucksakes,

Fucking *try,* Fuckhead,

Try.

EIGHTEEN

Thomas says "Good-bye" and then you wake up hangover-free—how delightful, how light—but the dream lingers and it was so vivid you want to stir your wife from sleep and accuse her of being a farmer's whore, to shake her at the shoulders and to give her a smack that would fill your alcoholic grandfather with pride—

But she's awake already—she beat you out of bed and that doesn't happen often. You can smell the coffee. It's weak, just how Wifey likes it.

She sits on the sofa in silence, reading; her phone's upside down on the coffee table next to her cup of java and her legs are stretched so that her feet overhang the couch's opposite arm. You go to give her a kiss, tell her you love her. She loves you, too. You are indescribably happy to hear that, so much so that you kiss her a second time, and *then* you help yourself to the coffee. It's the colour of chamomile tea and tastes like it was made with yesterday's beans.

Probably it *was* made with yesterday's beans.

Wifey can tell something's fishy, and it has nothing to do with her yeast infection.

She asks, "What's wrong?"

You tell her, without delving into specifics, that it was just a bad dream. She tells you that she had a dream that Boris was forty and had bought a log cabin in which he stored the bodies of murder victims.

And so on.

"Right," you say.

You head to the washroom for your morning whizz and send this text message to Gyles and Kilgore:

I fucked up, guys. I'm not able to come out and I'll have to pass on the job. I'll send you money for the plane tickets if you can't get a refund.

You feel sad, you flush the toilet, you toss your phone into your bedroom without a care as to where it lands, ensuring to turn it off before doing so because you don't want to know their reply. You head to your wife, kiss her for the third time of the morning. Being close to your wife makes it all go away, doesn't it? Her lips on your lips, your lips on her flesh, your bodies clasped together in a hug. Warmth unmatched.

“I love you,” you say to your wife.

“I love you, too,” she says.

Boris stirs, wakes.

NINETEEN

Today is Boris's first birthday.

Boris is one.

Can you believe it?

Yes, actually you can. Boris existed for a year, therefore Boris is one.

Congratulations.

Wifey has been preparing this day for the past five months. It's almost like today's a big deal. You have a beer after breakfast and tap glasses with your son who drinks apple juice from a Sesame Street sippie cup and then you have a second beer after your first beer because nobody's perfect.

Breakfast passes and by the end of it your wife is already scrubbing the colour out of all homely surfaces. Boris, perplexed, has a thing for making strange noises. He likes to blow fat raspberries. When he's blowing them a lot, you know he's happy; when he makes birdlike noises, you know he's excited; you know that "MAH!" is Mom, and "DAH!" is Dad. These days he's able to eat purees. He's upgraded from Human milk to Cow milk. You brush his four teeth twice a day and his poops are poops you wish to poop yourself—they're real wholesome and they clump together like fists in his Huggies. Probably you could use his droppings as baseballs.

A one-year-old is fun. They're nowhere near as fragile as their infantile selves. For example: they can fall from the sofa and bonk their head and cry for a bit but be fine; they can survive tumbles from their changing tables so long as they land a certain way, and shit, they can even take a spill down a set of stairs so long as they don't land on their noggins; you no longer see the pulse in their softspot. One-year-olds are tough little beasts—tougher than a lot of full-grown adults, really.

But:

The Birthday.

Your meager home has been rearranged in its entirety. Your sofa is pushed against the wall and you've borrowed a half-dozen folding chairs from your in-laws to make room for people you don't have room for. The cake has been baked and decorated with blue and orange frosting fit with a Hot Wheels F1 racer in the cake's center.

It's a good-looking cake; Wifey did it all herself. She's proud of it. You're proud of your wife.

A banner reads HAPPY BIRTHDAY! and it hangs on the wall behind the television; the kitchen table is covered with a cheap orange tablecloth and upon the table is a bowl of plain potato chips, a tall silver coffee pot—like the ones found at church luncheons—and a pile of Styrofoam cups and large punchbowl filled with what a punchbowl is supposed to be filled with: punch. You already feel claustrophobic even though you're not expecting guests for another two hours. These two hours pass like shit through a goose.

The party:

Imagine a sloth caught in a cold snap doused in cold molasses and told to climb a tree where all that awaits this sloth's arrival is the discovery that its wife has been cheating on him with a gorilla. This sloth will move slowly.

This is how the party goes.

You thought you knew noise until you were in a bourgeois house with a child of your own among an allotment of five other children ranging from Boris's age up to eleven with a lineup of a sister-in-law and six aunts and two grandmothers encouraging total tomfuckery whilst engaging in petty gossip and repetitious discourse. These women have yet to open the chardonnay. All the men are quiet, stunned. Each their beers are going flat; each of them wondering where they went wrong in their lives, where they can find the nearest emergency exit or parachute.

Somehow, someway, your father-in-law is asleep.

And so the party goes like this for hours but at least it doesn't appear that anybody has a cold. You're through with colds for a good while and wouldn't have a problem telling someone to fuck off with their snotty kid back to whatever infected hole they came from. Send sick children to the depths of their murky bedrooms and don't let them out until they're in the clear, you think. You begin dreading Boris's schoolyears and the endless lice infestations, and flus, and colds and strep throat and pinkeye.

"—ob?"

You ask, "What?" Your father-in-law has suddenly sprung to life. He stares at you.

"Have you heard more about the *job*?" He's speaking quietly, honouring your desires to keep the entire catastrophe on the DL.

"Refused it," you say, and your father-in-law reclines into the couch, closes his eyes once again and replies, "Good for you, son," and he closes his eyes and sleeps again.

Though slowly, this day passes. You're unable to drink that third beer and you were unable to drink the first two inside a half-hour because you're splitting referee duties with Wifey, who also has yet to leave the kitchen because she's working on…something—you don't know what she's working on because it doesn't look like she's working on anything, lo, there she is in the kitchen apparently doing *something.* Your mother-in-law is there while your own mother sits silently in the corner with your grandmother and an aunt because the other side of the family are a hurricane whereas the family you came from is the type of family to watch the hurricane around a hearth while drinking hot cocoa.

One of your nieces or nephews are accusing another niece or nephew of *not sharing*—

How fucking *dare* they.

You ignore them. It's best they figure it out on their own. They're not *your* kids, right?

Hell no they aren't—so fuck 'em, let 'em raise hell.

This bullshit is better than being single, though.

You make the best of it because your little man is a little less little and he gets a little less little with every even littler second.

TWENTY

Over a year into this blessed journey it strikes you that you hardly remember the first eleven months of Boris's life; it all blended together; all you remember is a hairless infant and a couple big leaky boobs. Now, somehow, Boris likes to fight you for the TV remote—oh, and while on this topic, you're stuck in the third season of Mad Men while having gone through Ready Steady Wiggle ten times last month on its own.

Boris grabs the remote and switches the source to HDMI 2. You ask him to return it.

"No!" he says.

"*Booooooorrrrrris….*"

He laughs because this is a joke to him. He begins pushing all the buttons he recognizes as buttons until he's returned to the source of your cable box and is surfing through On Demand movies. "Pick John Wick!" you urge, hoping with all hope.

Boris pauses for a moment as though, for only a moment, pondering the words you put forth—trying to piece them together in a way he can understand.

And then he puts on Ellen.

"Give me the fucking remote." You're serious now.

"No!"

"Yup!"

"No," Boris says, tugging hopelessly away then crying once you've removed it from his hands. He falls dramatically to the floor where he lies on his face like you just gored him with a greatsword. "My back hurts!" he says. "I broke my back!"

You remove the batteries before the crying gets too intense—before even a single tear falls. The little shyster is pretending to be as sad as he appears. You know the lines you can cross and the lines you *can* cross, but only should you do so with extra care.

"Say 'please,'" you say.

Boris looks at you dumbly.

"Please," you clarify.

And Boris says this:

"Dick!"

All right. You take this cuss as an intransitive verb that replaces the conventional *Please.*

You switch back to the game and give him the battery-less remote. Boris is happy. A happy Boris is a tolerable Boris even when your tolerance wanes, which is every day after work and whenever you want to get a couple of hours in for yourself. Luckily, it's Sunday, and the beer fridge is full; your mother bought you a bottle of Laphroaig 10 as a birthday present, you have yet to open it....

Wifey sits next to you and you can smell her feet. She's back to work and works weekends—you have Boris in the morning and then she gets home in the wee hours of the afternoon. Her feet smell like wet cheese. You can't tell her to take a shower because that's not how wives work. You begin using your shoulder as an inadequate filter. She begins telling you about her day but you can't hear what she's saying because her feet smell too loud.

"Really?" you say. You nod.

"Why is that so shocking?" Wifey counters.

You weren't listening so you can't muster a proper reply.

Fortunately: Boris. Your boy goes to Wifey, climbs up her knees and nuzzles into the crook of her elbow. Your wife kisses him a million times and by the end of this exchange the mini-you has been reduced to a sack of writhing giggles. He starts blowing raspberries and your wife blows one on his neck. You hear his diaper filling with urine. No—

You watch his diaper over*flow* with urine.

This is what aids your wife in deciding to shower. You had to suffer her putridity for only ten minutes but yet the taste lingers. She heads to the bathroom and Boris follows, who buck-nakedly sits on the bathmat playing with an empty shampoo bottle and your wife's noisome socks. The mountain of toys procured on his birthday gathers dust in his play-corner. Oh, how proud the partygoers were when Boris opened his gifts with glazed-over daft eyes, tired as fuck and oblivious to the goings-on. None of those gifts were meant for him as much as they were meant for the people who bought them so they could feel like they accomplished something more than just coming out to a birthday party.

There: I said it.

You spray a puff of Febreze and open the window. It's nice outside and the fresh air works wonders on your home's dank interior. You open the blinds and sunlight shines in and you feel alive. It's nice to feel alive; it's nice to stumble upon the reminder that a world goes by beyond the world of your own. You're not alone; your family isn't alone; Boris isn't growing up in a world where he'd be left alone to deal with the adventure that is childhood without a companion at his side, his very own Samwise Gamgee. This is a fond thought, and you breathe the springtime breeze, breathe it out, breathe it in....

"Dick!" Boris shouts from the bathroom. Wifey then counters with a stupefied and jocular, "WHAT?!"

"Dad Dick!" Boris shouts again — and then you realize he's trying to explain that you told him to put on John Wick.

These are the beginnings of a speaking toddler.

And the fun begins here.

TWENTY-ONE

You go to work and you come home and you go to work and you come home and you go to work and you come home and you go to work and you come home and Boris is *always* excited when you walk through the door.

Here's the problem:

He doesn't understand that you're tired.

On your way home, Ken suggests that you lollygag.

"Stop at the pub," Ken says. "Have a few pints—wings are half-off between four o' clock and six!"

Though tempting, you'd prefer a hot bath and a pint of Guinness; you'd rather get home, as exhausted as you are, to hold your boy for as long as your muscles allow before you begin nodding off on the sofa during the evening news while your boy wonders why you're not paying him any attention—though you hope he understands, at least slightly, why your eyes are as heavy as they are.

It's at a stoplight where you first realize that fatherhood is a lifelong challenge in which a man builds a child to be a person greater than himself. As a treat, you stop at McDonald's on the way home. Boris would enjoy a Happy Meal, surely. You get Wifey a couple Big Macs and fries. You'll eat whatever she leaves behind—that's how it's been working as of late, and you've found that in addition to the suppers and breakfasts you serve yourself you often wind-up finishing whatever's left on other plates. You figure you've gained ten pounds because your jeans are tighter than you've always known them to be. A gym membership seems appealing, but what time is there to exercise?

Listen:

You pull into your driveway and unbuckle your belt and exit your 2009 Dodge Caliber. It's still orange. You lock the doors, swing your backpack over your shoulder and make way to the front door and enter and you find a kid and couple of coots other than your wife in there and you'd prefer if they weren't there at all. Everybody looks at you as though you're intruding, nothing more than an inconvenience.

"Oh, my lovely Husband," your wife daintily starts. "You're home early."

"Wife," you say. "Who the fuck are these people and what are they doing in my fucking house?" You place your briefcase on the armoire and ignite a cigarette and set heading for your bar and you mix yourself a particularly stiff Old Fashioned there. You remove your blazer; you place it over the back of a dining room chair because it's your wife's job to hang it in your walk-in closet with all your other suits and exquisite alligator shoes. You remove your gold cufflinks, place them on the bar and then you roll your sleeves up to just before your elbows and you begin mixing a second beverage already:

Muddled sugar cube, orange zest, Angostura bitters, a handful of ice and then a 2oz pour of top-shelf bourbon.

Stir, stir, stir,

Stir,

Garnish with a maraschino cherry and a thin shaving of orange peel wiped around the rim of your crystal cup—your fucking regal *chalice*—to imbue your cocktail further with orange flavour, and then drink like you're Don Draper.

You're not.

You're just another asshole and sometimes your imagination gets the better of you.

In reality, you say "Oh, hi guys," with sincere surprise, and you know who these women are and unfortunately they have kids. By no means are they Tee Aitch Oh Em Eh Esses, but they're dirty little kids and they're running around your house like the assholes they are, all loud and stuff. One woman is your sister-in-law, and the other one is your wife's best friend, and the kids are hers.

"Your wife's gonna be my maid of honour," says your wife's friend who you've been fed-up with since about a week after meeting her. That was fifteen years ago.

"That's *wonderful,*" you say, and surely she can hear the italics on your voice but you couldn't care less.

"I want sweaty balls all over the place for my Bachelorette."

And so on.

"Even on my face and your wife's."

"Right."

You leave your backpack by the door, next to your shoes, and you retrieve a Budweiser from the cold, cold fridge.

Psst.

That's the beer opening. You drink it. You get another one, see your son sitting on the ground with his legs straight out with the wife's friend's kids. They're so fucking loud and you hope Boris isn't getting inspired.

Oh Thomas, you think.

Oh Thomas, you stinky fat fuck, please — please take me away.

You give Boris a kiss on a red cheek and make way to the shower regardless of your wife's friend asking why you're not kissing your wife. You run the water hot in hopes it puts you into a shock and that you die, but you don't.

Unfortunately.

You have another opportunity to kill yourself when you're shaving, but you don't because the sandalwood aftershave provides a sobering burn—you feel as clean as Baptist gash and soon clothe your legs with plaid pajama pants and your torso with the biggest and baggiest hoodie and your wife's friend simply *cannot* avoid commenting. Imagine her snide voice, the twang of her consonants and the sharpness of her vowels all of cutting through an otherwise warm house in a sudden icy gust and you'd love to cast a hand over her face but you'd never do that in front of children. This broad takes enough shit from her gym-going fiancé whose Gym is a popular one on the internet. They have a big house and a couple cars and a lot of money but ten times the debt to all their assets, cash included. You say nothing because she's offended enough by just living her life, and her kids are little rascals and nothing more and never could they ever be anything like Boris who's a goddamn angel able to keep quiet when all is loud.

This is what you do:

You fill a glass of water and sneak into your bedroom with intent to keep there until Wifey's visitors depart because your home is your castle and when you're through with a day you don't want to deal with bullshit, you want to return at the end of the day to your castle left as it was when you departed in the morning. The last thing you need to deal with at the end of the day are a pair of intruders and children to boot. No—

No no no.

Red-faced, you sit on your bed put your feet up and flick on Mad Men. You hear the din of female conversation, it penetrates the walls and the odd child's shout breaks them down, but you're tired, Fuckhead, and ten minutes into the fourth episode of Season Five your eyelids are shutting on their own volition and the sound of living room gossip is nothing compared this comfort which envelops you. Feel yourself falling into the crisp blankets on your clean skin, you smell your aftershave and you feel a breeze sighing over your face.

And then it's a sudden twenty-five minutes later and your wife bursts through the door asking you how your day was. Boris crawls in after her, starts towards the bed. You reach down and lift him up, plopping him next to you. His diaper looks like it's filled with two baseballs and a Georgia peach and you hear a squish when he sits.

You tell your wife how your day was; Boris is nattering in toddler-speak and he smells like your sister-in-law's three bichon frisés. You succumb to a sneeze, sip cold water from the glass next to you. Those two beers you drank less an hour ago remind you that you drank two beers less than an hour ago. You're groggy. It's seven o' clock. Wifey inquires about supper.

"No idea," you reply. You're telling the truth. You have no idea. No cravings.

In your queen-sized bed the three of you lay, Mad Men playing in the background while Boris makes sounds, as Wifey goes on about her sister and her friend and how they did this and how they did that and how one of their friends said that and how they replied *this* way or *that* way. To you, this is all white noise. Eventually your wife puts a pan on and starts frying ground beef for some spaghetti—a go-to in your household, and an excellent recipe that's been developed over the tenure of this relationship.

Boris-duty goes like this:

You sit on the living room floor as he stacks one block on another block, and upon an attempt with a third block this small tower comes crashing down and Boris cries. You plead that it's okay and that it takes time for things to work out but Boris's response are more cries.

And then *you* stack the blocks.

One. Two. Three.

Boris is delighted and you tell him that he did a wonderful job and that he's growing up and that in no way should he be in a rush to do that.

"Up!" Boris replies. "Gwow. Up!"

You say, "Terrible idea," and change the topic.

You rest against the sofa because Boris needs you sitting on the floor so he can fiddle with what he's fiddling: more blocks; the Wiggles are on the television and you've heard this song so many times you actually *like* when it comes around. You're tapping your foot as the room fills with caramelized notes of tomato sauce striking a pan, oregano, and black pepper and sea salt. Boris is peeing, you can hear it clearly, he doesn't move an inch as his diaper fills and it actually looks like he's smiling. This is a considerable pee, as it last upwards of the Wiggles' refrain of the chorus.

Do the propeller

Do the propeller

Do the pro-peller around and around!

And so on.

Your feet are tired from working through the day and your back is sore; you're still caught in the grog coming as a consequence from your two earlier beers and you're already thinking about what you'll make for breakfast the following morning. You're already due at work in twelve hours, and that's a dispiriting thought.

Twenty-five years to go, you think.

And so on.

Boris has got this all on his own; his block-stacking has improved greatly since you involved yourself—the little guy has piled *four* blocks on top one another and he's working on a fifth! Good for him, truly.

Unconsciously your eyes slide shut. You're not sleeping, but you're getting there. Your back's too sore to get shuteye on the floor, the noise coming from the kitchen is too great and surely Boris wouldn't appreciate his mentor taking a nap as he plays, leaving him to his own devices, including privileges to the remote control....

You find the secret spot in your position; the back of your head is nuzzled in the front of the crack of the sofa cushions. It's like you're wearing a neck brace, and this is nice. Your heartrate settles and all goes quiet, and then you're jolted awake by the sharp point of a block which has been cast into the center of your forehead.

Boris smiles jocularly; chubbily; innocently. You want to tell him to screw off but that feeling vanishes before you complete the thought. You reach over to him and poke him at the side of his ribs and he crumbles into a heap of laughs. You tickle him more and more until his laughs are so frequent they're one long scream. His smile is as wide as a smile can be as his hands clasp to your shock of hair, your shirt, your nose, but you keep tickling.

You stop.

Boris looks at you, disappointed.

And you resume tickling him.

And so on.

Supper's ready. It's 7:30 PM just as much as this is toddlerhood.

TWENTY-TWO

There is infancy and there is toddlerhood. Once you realize that your infant is a toddler, forget everything you've learned up until this point.

A toddler is a totally different animal.

This is where the test begins.

Ken comes around often because your focus wanes; Ken's aware that you feel inadequate through the day and that you long for peace and quiet at the end of your days. Ahead of you all you see is an endless calendar on which you'll roam, days and hours sloughing off your back like old skin as your child develops in a gloomy world with ordinary parents, living an ordinary life in an ordinary place when they live in a world that, these days, has no *room* for ordinary.

If you're average, you make enough to get by.

And this calendar stretches further than you're capable of seeing, and it ends, somewhere, and it's there where you'll simply *cease.* That's it, that's all. Ken hasn't changed a bit, unlike Boris, who these days needs more than you and Wifey can give....

Ken makes an intriguing argument:

"Work harder," he says.

I mean, it makes sense, right? By working harder you'll have discretionary income, you'd add a few extra bucks into your retirement accounts—and hey: you could retire earlier in spite of your surely worn-out back and extremities. At least, this is what Ken tells you.

You believe him and I can't blame you.

These days you accept Overtime whenever the opportunity strikes; you've worn out your work clothes to the point where there's hardly any clothes *left* to them and time flies because you work and your bank account swells like dead hooker slowly bloating yet rotting all at the same time.

Boris is eighteen months old and these days he eyes the toilet aplenty. When he's got to do his business he pauses, thinks, sometimes rises to scope the john but he never goes to it—no; oftentimes he'll stand outside the washroom and fill his diaper in the hallway. He thinks about the potty, and it's best you leave it at that—trust me, you don't want the guy getting scared of the big bad crapper; the big bad crapper is his friend, and you and Wifey acknowledge that, though longed for, this is a mountain to climb and to respect and that the day you don't have to change a diaper will be a day to celebrate and that's an event you'd rather not spoil because the champagne is ready and the corkscrew is in the depths of the cutlery drawer safe beneath a small purple spatula.

And so Wifey tells you about an upcoming family excursion to her parents' cabin that'll occupy she and Boris through the duration of the long weekend. You stand like a dunce where you stood when the news was broken and then your wife says,

"You can stay home if you want."

You're not sure what you want to do. A few days on your own could do you well, absolutely, but…there's something else there and you struggle to put your finger on it.

"So, you'll leave the Saturday morning," you say, "And you'll be back Monday afternoon?"

Your wife says that the plans would be to get back on the Monday, yes, and sometime after lunch. "You never know what my mom has planned," she goes further. "Might have a special lunch planned, who knows."

Right.

So you tell your wife that you'll think about it and let her know what you want to do in the coming days—the long-weekend is still a ways' away, and you have a week of work ahead, Overtime included.

Boris dances stiff-legged in the living room, bracing himself on the TV stand, his diaper jiggling as he shifts. He's just squatting more than anything else, but you get the point; it's cute. You open YouTube on your phone, select something appealing and once the sound begins he pauses his tango and waddles towards you.

"Wha's thah?" he asks.

"YouTube," you reply.

Boris snatches the phone from your hand, laughing while he does so and heads to sit in the corner next to this bookshelf which contains a wide selection of Dr. Seuss and Robert Munsch. He has a small rocking chair there, and he sits in it with the phone in his lap. You watch your boy intently, the video you had going was a simple compilation of various Fails—usually people falling on their faces or fat people tumbling off tables.

This is Boris's first taste of drugs.

You're now raising an addict, and there's no rehab for this ominous affliction.

TWENTY-THREE

Aside from "Mom," or "Dad," the next word Boris hits on the head is "Tablet."

And then that quickly devolves to, "Wawn my tablet," which goes among Boris's first sentences.

But at least the thing keeps him quiet; it's added to his vocabulary, thanks to YouTube Kids, and he's learning how to fiddle around with the simplest of games. He also enjoys staring at himself in the camera, the vain little stinker—you don't have a problem with this as long as he's not trying to perfect the art of the selfie or scrolling ass-pics on Instagram.

Now, the OT you've been working has caught up to you. You lay in bed in the mornings for an extra fifteen, even twenty minutes, and add an extra scoop of ground Dark Roast to the French Press. Coffee goes down smoother and you're up to three cups before seven o' clock, and then you're on the road again for another eight to eleven hours. Somewhere in the middle of that you'll stop for a Red Bull to wash down your lunch and then an iced coffee to wash down the Red Bull. Caffeine's affects are minimal. Your next best hope for extra energy will be an improved diet: less alcohol, an extra serving of vegetables at dinner and an apple or a banana instead of four bacon slices at breakfast. A man's gotta do what a man's gotta do.

"Burgers," says your wife. Boris is tight in your hands and he's pressing his head firm into your breast. You kiss his head; you tell him you love him. "Homemade fries, too." Wifey gestures to the Lodge pot on the stove, filled with three inches of peanut oil. Next to the Cast Iron is a platter of fried potatoes which glimmer under a coat of oil and sea salt which shimmer under the incandescent kitchen light like they're diamonds. Your house smells like a cheap diner.

"I'll have half a burger and five fries," you say. The fries are big—you could easily consider them potato wedges.

Your wife looks at you like there's an albatross on your head.

"Do we have low-fat mayonnaise?"

"…."

"And the buns: they aren't brioche, are they?"

They definitely are; you can tell by how they're brown and shiny.

You have half a burger and five fries, skipping the mayo, and then you help yourself to the other half and whatever fries your wife doesn't eat, which, it turns out, was the lion's share of them. You're bloated on the couch until you shit hours later, and then you go to sleep.

Wake up; lounge twenty minutes in bed; tug on a pair of sweats, add an extra tablespoon of coffee to the press; drink it; drink four cups altogether; brush your teeth; head to work. Today you'll take Ken's advice seriously. You plan to skip lunch. A good twenty-four hour fast is what you need, something to reset the gut—*this* will give you that needed energy, that energy which you crave, which your wife and son deserve.

Clyde and Brianne, either considerably high and smelling boldly of the devil's lettuce, ask you to pull into the Golden Arches for your lunchbreak. "Go on in," you say to them. "My wife's got a big dinner planned, want to save my appetite." And so Clyde and Brianne head in and return with three bags of food. They buy four Double Cheeseburgers and two Egg McMuffins for the pair of them. "We'll have some extra fries, Driver," Brianne says to you. You say nothing. You drink water until your stomach's had its fill.

A half-hour later: "What's this special dinner you've got planned?" Clyde asks.

You're not entirely sure what he's talking about so you say, "Probably grilled cheese and tomato soup—something easy to whip-up when Wifey's alone with the kiddo."

"You said you were having a big dinner, though…."

You've been caught red-handed. "Shit," you say, laughing a trifle. "What day is it?"

It's Wednesday.

"Shepherd's pie."

"Shepherd's pie?" Clyde retorts.

"Shepherd's pie," you affirm. "It's *excellent* when you shred a handful cheddar on top the potatoes. A little cheesiness goes a long way."

Clyde and Brianne eat their McDonald's. Neither of them would know a good Shepherd's Pie one were put on a table before them. You work five hours longer, taking you to ten hours by the time you clock-out. Your next paycheque should be a fat one, the OT you've logged has been considerable. You could start supplementing your diet with a green smoothie or something along the lines. Probably you could find a couple good recipes on YouTube.

"Lasagna," says your wife. Home smells *delectable* and you're so famished you could eat the fucking paint off the walls.

Ravenous, you eat a slice in a flash, and then you eat the caesar salad with croutons which supplement the lack of crunch—the leaves are a touch wilted, as it's apparent they've been doused in sauce for a while. It's good, though. Still in your work clothes you grab a beer, drink it in a blink, and then you help yourself to a second slice.

Your fast has ended. You deserve this, you think.

And then, for a third slice, you have a half-slice. You're controlling yourself; this is *great;* these are habits worth building, oh yes they certainly are. You peel off your work clothes and then hop in the shower. Boris sits on the floor and fiddles with a toy that squeaks and pops and entertains him amid his daily technology break. You wash your ass, your balls, your pits and nooks and crannies and then you shave what stubble has appeared over the past bit. You smack your face with aftershave and Boris gets a laugh outta that—it sounds like this:

"A-ha-huck-huck-huck-huck-haaaa!"

He usually laughs until he starts coughing. This is how you know he's good and entertained. You sit on the couch; Boris sits *next* to you on the couch. The Evening News reminds you that the world still isn't the happiest, but *fuck* the world—you're happy within these four walls, and you your wife and Boris love one another. That's all that matters.

Boris starts moving his legs when you're dozing off, and his feet often kick your plonker. Your underpants are snug around your thighs and plums and you have bad gas. "Can you go sit with your mom for a bit?" you ask your little man. He refuses, and then your wife puts forward the idea that you should cut back on the OT for a couple of weeks.

"Recover is all," she says. "It'll be nice to have dinner around five again."

"But we need more money," you say.

And then your wife asks, "Why?"

You stare beyond the television and out the window thinking about how to answer your wife's reasonable inquiry. The answer should come easy, and through your head run reasons such as inflating your support; reinforcing your nest; money to use towards the end of your working years so you can retire peacefully,

But you struggle in getting beyond the harsh reality that gone are the days of Defined Benefit pensions and 1% inflation; gone are the days of sure-returns and affordable livings; gone are the days of certainty, dare you consider it, and that you're hardly any different than the asshole whose dog just pinched one out on your front lawn.

Your answer is this:

You want *more.*

Ken wants more.

But you can't say this to your wife because it's unfair, so you say nothing at all.

TWENTY-FOUR

Later that evening, next to your wife in bed, you say to Ken, pleading:

"You gotta help me out here, man," but Ken isn't sure what you mean.

You tell Ken that his desires are vague, but Ken tells *you* that it's up to *you* to figure out what your desires *are*.

You disagree with Ken, but he insists.

You still disagree.

Ken says nothing. He waits, expecting you to come around, but you're waiting, too—just like he is. It is quiet.

"Are you coming with us to the cabin?" Wifey asks—Ken skitters off into the dark and stays there.

"I don't think so," you tell your wife. You tell her you have some stuff to work out. Afterall, tomorrow is only Thursday, therefore you have two days and a couple of hours left to make your decision.

Ken looms in the corner, a shadow awaiting the chance to infiltrate your dreams.

And he meets you there.

TWENTY-FIVE

You contemplate murder today.

This is why:

Boris starts crying at 4:00 AM on the nose—complete wailing, in fact—and you tear from your room like a bullet from its chamber and lash open his door and his cries cease, he looks at you all wide-eyed and such as though having been disturbed, and then he *really* starts crying.

He's all yours now, Fuckead.

It's 4:01 AM.

Your wife says through the bedroom door, "He was probably just having a bad dream."

Yeah, probably she's right, but rising to a howling child is far from a soothing way to wake. Boris may very well have been being kidnapped!

Nonetheless, Good morning; nice to see you and your swollen eyes, bags beneath them, and quite purple to boot. It looks like you and the Sandman got into a tussle and that you came outta the other end worse for wear.

Despite being shocked at your sudden arrival, Boris is delighted to see you. Look at that smile, those chubby cheeks and his full diaper. Isn't it odd how full diapers are kind of cute? You give Boris a kiss and then you make your coffee, promising to return with a bottle.

Boris feeds.

You are the feeder now.

Boris spits-up and what runs down your wrist is warm and chunky, thin oatmeal. Defying gravity it runs up your leg and into the canal that is your ass crack. Your buttocks glide over one another as though either has been lathered in KY as you fetch a burp cloth and a handful of Kleenex. Boris's face is wiped, your ass is, too, and then it's The Wiggles until you arrive on Sesame Street, which is two hours away.

Suuuuunnny days, sweepin' the,

Cloooooouuuddsss awwaaaaaaay!

And so on.

It will never leave your head.

You eat toast and jam and brew yourself a cup of coffee but no matter what you put into your body the energy required for a toddler at the sub-five o' clock -hour is unattainable.

Boris brings you a soccer ball, asks to go for a car ride.

"Not gonna happen," you say.

Boris insists.

"Still not gonna happen."

Boris cries.

You soothe him; you drink your coffee, eat your toast.

"Wawn my tablet," says Boris. He gets his tablet, asks for a snack. You get him dry Cheerios. He spills the Cheerios, cries. He doesn't want them anymore and gets mad when you eat them.

"No *I* wawn them," he says. You return Boris's Cheerios; he doesn't touch them. They wind up in the garbage by the time your wife wakes up, which is around seven, but it's not yet five.

Embrace the waste.

It's five o' clock now; you're three episodes into deeper Ready Steady Wiggle and you're feeling no wigglier than you did when you woke up. You're stiff with anger and frustration and the fact that Boris is gung-ho and ready to go is stifling.

Oh, the pleasures of not yet being in the workforce.

Boris's back doesn't squeak like an old tire swing when he sits; his feet don't hurt when he walks; his knees don't crack when he bends. What a good life he has, living it to the fullest and even waking up earlier than the majority of folks do, soaking in the maximum amount of the day, experiencing what *is* to take into tomorrow, to attain maximum amounts of what *will* be.

You feel like a real asshole when you realize that Boris has both television privileges and his tablet.

Hell no.

You wield the remote with shielded intentions, exit Netflix.

Boris doesn't realize.

Yet.

And you open the Guide; you peruse the PVR, HBO, STAR; you skim the Adult Channels and laugh at the names you find there.

Creaming, is one; *Salamander,* is a second; *Big Black Dicks in Bigger White Chicks,* is another—a *classic.* In the name of equity, then follows *Medium White Dicks in Medium Black Chicks.* Lots of dicks and chicks.

Chuckling you continue through the guide and settle on the Morning News—you've really familiarized yourself with this cast and have even sent in a birthday greeting for your wife a couple birthdays ago. She loved it, and then the News went on to talk about a Terror Attack which claimed the lives of fifteen innocents—

What better ways to wake up are there aside from the News?

The Weatherman says "A storm's a-comin'!" and he gestures to a low-pressure system rising from the south to devour your town for lunch. According to the Weatherman this storm will blow things around for two days before the sun shines again, which means there will be less OT at work—not an entirely bad thing. A break doesn't sound terrible—you're tired of work anyways, and work's tired of you; maybe you should just quit and buy a hut in Thailand, never work again, drink Thai booze on beach on the daily and acquire an opium habit, lose ten pounds, possibly perfect a bone-broth….

Boris is offended that you've turned off Netflix.

"Tablet or the TV," says you.

Boris disagrees; says, "No!" and pushes his tablet off his lap. It falls to the floor and he cries.

You think, *Good job,* and retrieve your little man's tablet because you're a good dad and don't want him running around. Your goodwill goes unrecognized—

Get used to it—

Because the tablet finds its way to the floor once again. In an toddleresque way Boris shares that his orneriness is in no way shape or form due to the hour of his waking and exclusively because you turned off The Wiggles.

You will not allow Boris to Wiggle while he watches his tablet.

"One thing at a time," you say. You tell him that he'll get a headache and that television and a dancing Australian girl dressed in a yellow dress fit a yellow bow are *definitely* not worth crying over. "You're too young to have a crush," you say. "Plus, Emma's married to that skinny guitar player." You think his name is Oliver but truly you couldn't give half a nut—his name could be Charles Manson for all you care, you just want to sit on the couch and get in twenty minutes of shuteye; the same would do Boris wonders, but he's far from being in the mood.

Boris spills from the sofa and toddles over to his Play Corner and finds his blocks there, and then he finds his action figures and a stack of board books and a large puzzle that you're able to solve with your eyes shut. Boris wants to do the puzzle.

"I'll be right there," you say, but you don't really mean it—really you're hoping that Boris acknowledges your willingness and that he goes on to forget about it, but he's fooled by nothing. He sees through the bullshit, says "Daddy sit!"

"Be right there," you say. "Gonna make some more coffee first."

"Okay," says the little man. "Ready now?" he says seconds later.

"Five minutes."

Boris sighs. "Okay," he says. You stand by the kettle as the water boils, your home is silent. You spin around to see Boris standing in the kitchen's cusp, asking to be held. You give him a hoist, kiss his cheek, tell him you love him. He loves you, too.

"Ready now?" he asks.

"Almost," you say. "Couple minutes."

And then you smell his soiled diaper. You ask him if he's pooped.

Boris says no.

You attempt a peek through a diaper leg-hole—you're fought off, Boris wriggles away. You don't even need to check—you know the smell of your son's shit like a sailor knows their stars. Some folks you went to high school with have six-figure jobs, and there's you: an expert in your offspring's refuse.

You say, "Gotta change your bum, big guy."

Boris fights your words and initiates reeling cries in the style of devil-worshipping black metal and warmth leaks down the side of you to which Boris clings and you think

Change the fucking diaper

Right

Now

Because this fucking kid is pissing on me

So you lay a pair of tea towels on the living room floor and place Boris upon them; his body is taught and lifting his legs to remove the diaper without smearing his ass with feces is to lift his entire body with his neck as the fulcrum; his cries go muted and you lift his bottom to remove his diaper with minimal mess but he pees again and the yellow spurts outta his penis like water from a cherubim fountain—the stream arches and splatters on his face. He gargles his urine like mouthwash, gags; you lift him up, pat his back until he stops coughing and you then resume changing him. His cries resume and you wonder how your wife has slept through this for Boris's howls are considerable—formidable. You feel self-conscious within the walls of your own home and fully expect to peer through a window to find your mother there like Tobe Hooper from Stephen King's 'Salem's Lot prepared to enter and to suck your blood.

You remove the shit-holster and slide it to your right and fill it with a dozen baby wipes before folding it shut—it stays that way, thanks to the gluey poo.

Like *spackle*, you recall.

Spackle.

Your own poopy toilet paper clung to the shower's tiling.

Like spackle.

You laugh under your breath at your wife's misfortune and your own forgetfulness.

These lighthearted moments are what get you through the heavier ones.

By the time you have Boris re-diapered and placed on the couch, you hear him already refilling it—probably from the milk he drank first thing. Impressive, you think. What an outstanding metabolic rate!

You might be raising a pro-athlete! but you doubt it, highly. If your sore back and bad feet and crackling kneecaps are any indication of Boris's sporting future, the poor dude's utterly boinked.

You work on the same puzzle from five-fifteen to six o' clock because Boris doesn't understand them just yet and he gets all the praise despite the fact that it's you who's done the puzzle nine times wire-to-wire; you know the Paw Patrol through-and-through and you hate them already.

Cloudy days are swept away at six. Hooray!

Thank Christ for that little red pervert called Elmo, for he has Boris rapt with interest and keeps his attention until seven when Wifey emerges from the bedroom at last with her tattered black gotch wedged about a mile up her intergluteal cleft. "Long morning?" she asks. You nod.

Boris falls asleep fifteen minutes later within Wifey's arms. You're due at work in an hour and you have yet to eat breakfast and to take your morning constitutional.

You wash your hands after this, a few slices of bacon sizzling in the kitchen, your wife scrambling some eggs for your omelette.

Ken returns your gaze as you look into the mirror. He says, "You can walk away from this any time you want."

You ignore him.

You wouldn't change this for the world.

Ken's gotta go, you think, and you got the weekend all to yourself—

The perfect opportunity to commit murder.

TWENTY-SIX

Buckhalter Peterson is a friend of yours. The pair of you worked at a restaurant some years ago and became friends there.

You say to Buckhalter, "Buckhalter?"

And Buckhalter says, "Yes, Fuckhead?"

"I want to kill half of myself," you say.

"Hmm," hums Buckhalter. "Met Ken, have you?"

"Indeed," you reply.

"I thought so," says Buckhalter.

And that was that exchange.

Buckhalter is a father of three.

Three.

A boy of nine and a pair of four-year-old girls—they're twins. Oftentimes he says, "No one in their right mind would plan for three kids—three's a very accidental number," he says. "I would've stopped at two, but, you know…shit happens."

Buckhalter is an amazing father but he didn't get to where he is without his share of struggles. He's imperfect, as all humans are, and at times he gets down on himself about that. Some nights he'll sit in his recliner and drink whiskies until sleep takes him—but once, it was worse.

At one point it was *much* worse.

"Ken's the guy who shows up at the party thinking he's the shit and then he donks the girl with the cold sores, wakes up with a pus-dick and a scarlet rash to boot," says your friend named Buckhalter. "The guy almost ruined my life."

"How'd you get rid of him?" you inquire.

"Can't say I ever did," says Buckhalter. "At least, not all of him."

You think, *You hide it well,* and then you bite a tuna sandwich. You took no OT this rainy day and your day was cut short—thank God for salary. The restaurant the pair of you converse in teems with shadow and your waitress is a smoker who wears enough makeup to add a couple years. You figure she's seventy-three and you know that for a fact because her gravelly voice is a chainsaw.

Like Cookie Monster the waitress growls “Cooooooffffffeeeee?” According to her nametag, her name is

Nobodyfuckingcaresshesonlyhereforacoupleparagraphs.

You and Buckhalter slide her your cups. You drink more coffee, ask more questions.

You ask Buckhalter what he does when Ken comes around.

“I acknowledge him, that’s for sure,” Buckhalter begins. “I discovered that if you ignore him he’ll just come back around with excess motivation. That’s what happened back in ‘17.” Apparently Buckhalter is too busy to mutter all the syllables.

2017, you think. What a wild year….

“To acknowledge the guy all I do is a little bit of a stupid thing.”

“Like…?” you encourage.

“I usually go to the pub down the road from my place on a Tuesday or Thursday and get some cheap beer and wings, get a little drunk and admire the server’s legs and thick rump.”

“Rump?”

“Ass.”

You know; you get it. You appreciate a good thick bottom.

"And that's enough?" you say, taken aback—you expect this to be about as satiating to Ken as it is to drink a mug of chicken boullion to quench your thirst.

But Buckhalter says, "Oh yeah," with inspiring surety. "There's nothing more unappealing to a good looking and fit young woman than watching a dude indulge in beer and half-price wings in a work uniform while he plays Temple Run on a beat-up iPhone 8."

You flutter your eyebrows at this sobering epiphany.

"It's important that you *humble* Ken," Buckhalter goes on. "The dude knows no humility—the guy might as well be Mandingo."

"You still play Temple Run?"

"Great game," says Buckhalter. "Best game that's ever graced a phone screen."

You nod in agreement and then pay the bill.

The waitress snarls, "Thank-you, loves; come again!"

And you board your 2009 Dodge Caliber and start home.

Your 2009 Dodge Caliber is still orange.

Thick-rumped waitresses scatter.

TWENTY-SEVEN

Ken says, "Remember, it's not all about sex, man."

"I have my doubts," you reply.

Ken says that he just wants what's best for you.

"How?" you ask. "In what way? Be specific."

Ken says that he wanted you to double your salary with Gyles and Kilgore so you could provide for your family—so you could provide for them twice as much as you already do. Ken says that you could've been wealthy should you have accepted that position. "In more than money," he says. "It was your *dream* job," he says.

You tell Ken that you couldn't uproot your family.

"Sometimes spouses just don't understand," says Ken. "Sometimes it's gotta be you who takes the initiative."

You shake your head.

"No wonder you're damned to the middle-class," says Ken. "You get what you deserve."

You shake your head and the car goes silent. Home is three left-hand turns away; the weekend between you and your worst enemy begins tomorrow and you've yet to produce a plan. What information you gained from lunch with Buckhalter was woeful, to say the least. What you took from that was that you have to find some half-price wings and Miller Lite, but the problem is that there's no fucking way you can find half-price wings on the weekend.

You ask me if I'm kidding you.

I'm not. Half-price wings on the weekend would be total madness.

Madness!

MADNESS!

An early supper is ready when you get home. Boris sits in his highchair with Wifey at the table and there's a pot of steaming short-rib ragout in the table's center with an empty plate sitting opposite your wife. You already look forward to Monday—the end of a long weekend that will be *too* long. You plant kisses on both your wife and son and eat supper. Before long, the day is through and a new one begins.

And so on.

TWENTY-EIGHT

Standing upon the precipice of a life-changing weekend an ominous wind purls through your home.

You'll be a murderer come Tuesday, should you survive.

With an arm behind your pillow you lay next to your slumbering wife and mutter "I love you" and you kiss her cheek; you massage her shoulder and say "I love you" again in case she didn't hear the first time round.

She's sleeping—she didn't hear you because you spoke quiet enough to keep her from waking up.

Whatever.

Work flies by as though nothing important happened—and this is the case indeed. You return home to find Wifey stuffing a small suitcase with sundresses and socks and shorts and tees and her favourite pajamas and it hits you that tonight will be your first night alone in *years.* Yeah, there had been a couple nights you'd dozed on friends' sofas after bibulous eves, and your wife has had a couple of her own, but this is the first time where you'll go to sleep one night and wake up the next morning all on your pitiful lonesome. It already feels strange. Tonight there will be no 3:00 AM entrances, no stumbles through the kitchen and down the hall into a cold shower and then into a bed—from either party—no; tonight you're alone and you'll go through tomorrow all the same.

Boris eats thin apple slices dusted with cinnamon in his highchair, imbibing himself with his tablet. Peppa Pig. You like Peppa Pig; there's something cozy about Peppa Pig that you can't put your finger on. Probably it's their English accents, often-talk of tea and George's dinosaur.

Rawr!

Boris drools as he looks at the screen, a goddamn junkie.

"Hi, Boris," you say.

Boris doesn't say chipperly, "Greetings, father!" He's too high for that—totally distracted. He doesn't know you're there. His drool-string lengthens, touches the top of his breast as your wife fills a small Yeti cooler with a bottle of white wine, a pack of a dozen Schneider Wieners, a bottle of mustard and a bottle of ketchup; you take a peek inside the cooler, a dozen yogurts are in there among a package of bottled water, apples, oranges, grapes and a fifth of tequila. You can't help but ask, "Gonna get fucked up?"

"It's for Webster."

"Webster?" you quip.

"Yes," says your wife. "Webster Lockhart."

"Ah." You breathe easily. Webster Lockhart is your brother-in-law.

You stand looking out your bay-window over your traffic-calmed neighbourhood with this on your mind, and weighing heavily is the stark fact that you're the only member of the family staying back as the rest go out to celebrate nothing at all but an extra day off. You figure this is hardly anything worth celebrating given that a single day is but a drop in the bucket when you have upwards of twenty years to deal with before the endless weekend comes—if it comes at all. You offer Wifey your help and she tells you to carry everything to the front door and to fetch a pair of Boris's stuffies. You put Sally Periwinkle beside the Yeti Cooler, and his favourite cat Stu the Perv on top of Sally Periwinkle.

You stand in your work clothes as Wifey puts the finishing touches on her outgoing luggage and she says to Boris, "Up, time to go for a car ride to the cabin."

"No!" Boris counters, and he opens his mouth and out comes a stray Cheerio.

"We'll get you some nuggets for the drive."

"Okay!" Boris says excitedly. Raising a man of reason, you are. Wifey plucks his tablet from his highchair as you lift him from his seat, take him to the doorstep and you sit him down there. He enjoys putting his shoes on and he always smiles through this process. Your house already seems quieter, a looming loneliness spread heavily throughout.

Sister-in-law pulls up out front and Wifey bursts into frenetic haste, panicking as though afraid that she and Boris will be left behind. She peels through the front door with the Yeti in one hand and her bag and Boris's in the other. The hatchback trunk of your sister-in-law's Crossover sways open and in it your wife stores the luggage. You then hear her say to her sister, "He's not coming." You can practically see your sister-in-law rolling her swampy eyes—you give about as many shits as the noontime-hour when very few shits are taken at lunch.

"You be a good boy for Mom," you say to Boris, you kiss the tip of his nose and he giggles, says "Okaaaayyyy," and comes in for a hug. You hug him; he hugs you.

"Daddy's gon come," Boris says.

"Daddy's staying home," you reply, and it hurts a touch. "I have to kill somebody," you say, and then you wink. "Just kidding," you say, even though you're dead serious.

Boris releases the same “Okaaaayyyy” as earlier, but this time with a downward inflection which mimics the frown on his face. You give him another hug—this one even tighter than the last.

“I’ll be here when you and Momma get back, I’m looking forward to it. Go have fun with Winchester and Emilio.” Winchester and Emilio are Boris’s cousins. You whisper to Boris, “And when you get home in a couple days, maybe we can order a couple pizzas and watch a movie, all right?”

“Okaaaayyyy!” He’s excited now. “Bye-bye, Daddy!”

“Bye-bye, my boy. Be good.”

TWENTY-NINE

The incredible weight of loneliness falls upon your shoulders in a wave out of nowhere before you sister-in-law steers her vehicle around the corner and out of sight. You never experienced silence until this moment, and you're not sure you like it. It's five o' clock, and at the turn of the hour you still find yourself pacing a lifeless living room.

You tell yourself that this tranquility will last only three days before your home is loud again, yourself again longing for peace and quiet by Monday evening when Boris and Wifey return reeking of campfires and dogs and bedsheets that are not their own—a foreign aroma, sweat-of-the-many.

Will Boris sleep? you wonder. Will your wife be kept up through all hours of the night as Boris stirs in a bed that isn't his, ruffling the sheets and tugging them from your wife? Will Boris eat the breakfasts put in front of him, or the lunches or the dinners? Will Boris know how to swim when your mother-in-law takes him into the lake and says "Swim, Boris! Swim, you little fucker!" or will he sink? Will your father-in-law make beef stroganoff on a scorching July afternoon, or will he try his hand at a jalapeño gazpacho? Will Boris be expected to eat these foods he has never tried?

Likely.

"What the *fuck* have I done?" you ask an empty house. You feel like something has been ripped outta the middle of your chest and there are no chances of seeing it again until late Monday afternoon less you saddle-up in your orange Dodge Caliber, made in 2009, and fall in the wake of the loves of your life out into lake country where everything will smell of woodsmoke and ice cream and propane barbecues manned by drunken caucasoids who think they can cook.

You ring the pizzaman and say "A double pepperoni with extra sauce, please, and a chicken bacon mushroom with ranch."

The pizzaman says, "Would you like a drink?"

"Diet Coke, please," you say. "I'm watching my weight."

The pizzaman says, "Right," and the wait begins. You get in an episode of Mad Man while crushing two pints of Guinness, and then the pizza arrives. Five minutes later you receive a text from Wifey noting that they'd arrived safely and that they found a dead raccoon in the firepit.

You tell your wife to send you a photograph and soon you behold the expired forest creature: without a doubt it's the deadest thing you've ever seen; it's bloated to the point where a pin could pop it and the thing nearly fills the firepit. It looks like a big pillow.

And then you vanquish a slice of the pepperoni, and then a slice of chicken bacon mushroom ranch, and then you help yourself to a third pint of Guinness. Tonight your flatulence will be formidable—probably it's for the best that you're alone. In place of a fourth beer you drink the Diet Coke—it's too late to get drunk on your own, your alcohol tolerance is no longer what it once was. Ken keeps quiet, he lets you drink your Diet Coke in peace.

And so this is your night. By no means is this anything remarkable but in no way are you down on yourself. This is fatherhood on its own; this is fatherhood when there's no work to tend to nor family to occupy your attention. You're focused full bore on the television and Don Draper and the wonders of Diet Coke and four slices of pizza. Less than an hour later your heart races from alcohol consumption and all that pizza and Diet Coke. You drink water and strip off your pants and now you pace your living room in loose boxer shorts with balls a-flappin' and the breeze is nice down there. Renewing.

This is your night, Fuckhead.

Eventually, you sleep.

THIRTY

For a proper Frittata, one needs eggs. You have eggs—plenty.

Here is the recipe for a Mediterranean Frittata:

Preheat oven to 350°.

Dice one small red onion and a green pepper. Add diced onion to a pan lightly oiled with extra-virgin olive oil; season with salt and pepper and sweat the onion until translucent.

While onions sweat, lightly whisk six eggs in large bowl, add a splash of milk and a dollop of soft salted butter. When onions are adequately sweated (translucent), add green pepper and whole cherry tomatoes to pan with chopped oregano. Season with salt and pepper. Add eggs to the pan, stir; stir in the eggs from side of pan the ensure consistency. Add large chunks of feta.

Place pan in heated oven and cook for fifteen minutes.

Serve immediately.

That is how you make a frittata. I'm sure you know how to eat a frittata, but in case you don't, this is how to eat a frittata:

Put a forkful in your fucking mouth.

Chew and swallow.

Repeat.

That is how you eat a frittata.

You're making a frittata for breakfast, labouring atop a hot stove with the window above the oven open and sucking your good cooking out. Your penis is shrunk this morning, recovering from intense morning wood, but don't worry, it's growing. Blood spreads through your body like a river cresting its banks as you shift about; blood fills your arms, your legs, and yes, your nethers. Ken will keep hidden while you're in this vulnerable state, all tiny-dinked and such. You ask Ken if he'll come out and play and you twirl the 8" chef knife. Ken says nothing. You don't complain, though today, murder is on your mind—tantamount to this here frittata.

Orange juice; a glass of a tomato juice; a glass of water to boot. You take a cup of coffee with you to the couch where you'll await your nemesis's arrival. Two episodes of Mad Men pass before you realize that Ken's nowhere to be seen—you can't hear him either.

What is it? you wonder, watching your TV but not really watching it. Why isn't Ken coming around?

You call for Ken but Ken doesn't come; you don't so little as hear your own echo, your mind is an all-consuming abyss from which nothing is able to escape. It's leftover pizza for lunch, thirty situps with thirty mirrored pushups, and a liter of water. And then you have a beer.

It's only lunch, and it was an early lunch.

Your phone dings, a text from Buckhalter.

Kill him yet?

You haven't, and you share this with trusty ol' pal.

Lunch? Buckhalter asks. He also offers to pick you up. He drives a Dodge Ram.

Sure.

It's always nice when you don't have to drive. You change into presentable clothes and Buckhalter arrives by one. Lunch is enjoyed at an old stomping ground of yours and your friends'—it's downtown, across from the place where all the good concerts take place, home of the local pro hockey team. Plenty of ass was had based out of this fun-hub and you've enjoyed countless pints here—most of which not remembered due to an early-twenties whisky-haze.

Buckhalter compliments your shirt.

"But I always wear this shirt," you say.

"It suits you," says Buckhalter.

Your ego finds its wings, but you restrain yourself. "Thanks, Buckhalter."

"You're welcome, Fuckhead."

Buckhalter rambles about his past week and brings up memories of old—memories from before either of you were married with kids. You're both working on local craft beers to the sound of a classic Celtic-punk playlist that stirs your adrenaline. You think about the Dropkick Murphys show you went to a year-and-a-while back—you watched that broad hopping up and down in her kilt-like miniskirt, her cosmopolitan cocktail spilling from the top of her plastic rocks glass fit with a tiny black straw. What a fun night, you think, also recalling the sensation of wanting to get home but at the same time wishing you never felt that feeling at all, leaving you to be as you wanted to be, kind of like how you are right now, but three times worse because there's nothing to rush home to....

The beer is the cause of these thoughts. Buckhalter orders you a gin and tonic to match his. You bite a deep-fried dill pickle and there's an explosion of flavour. The waitress swings by, places a flyer face-down on the table and inquires if you guys would like another round of food. Though you're hungry, you decline another order of food—you don't want to bloat more than you already are and the night is still young; the night is so young that it's not yet even the evening.

You view the flyer and discover that it advertises tonight's entertainment: a local band is scheduled to play—a funk band—with three opening acts. Bands hit the stage at nine and draughts of Heineken are on special. Cover's $5. This concert is 70s-themed.

"I don't know shit about the seventies," you say.

"Waitress," says Buckhalter to the spry young'un, who looks to your friend with a smile.

"Yes, patron?"

"Are you familiar with any good thrift shops?"

"Thrift shops?" the waitress copies. "Why, of course I do. I have a thrifting side hustle where I sell tattered bullshit to fools like myself for hundreds of dollars!

"Pssh," the waitress says, waving a hand as though telling Buckhalter to get out of town. "Who *doesn't* know about good thrift shops?"

And then she goes on explaining where to find them. It turns out that there are three within a twenty-minute radius from the pub.

And so you go thrifting for '70s apparel at the closest Goodwill. There you find a large blond afro and a pair of bell-bottom jeans that are tight on the sack and a satin button-up littered with sequins. On its breast are two landing-strips of trim. You do the buttons up halfway and leave to rest to the imagination. Everything about your garb is '70s except for your Chuck Taylor shoes, you're fine with this.

Buckhalter looks like Wolfman Jack and he leads you into the pub strutting with a sway to his shoulders he's never had before. This isn't the Buckhalter you know, this is something entirely different and you're *inspired,* so you mimic his swagger with a sway of your own and nobody looks at you because still their greasy pub-fare is more appealing than you and your friend. You and Buckhalter pull up seats at the bartop.

"Love the outfits, boys," says the bartender who's a man with cannons for biceps. They're vascular and large. You and Buckhalter each order beers, you drink them fast and order a couple more. You're undoubtedly buzzing hard already and you and your pal are the only two dressed for the show. You two fit in like a couple of Black Panthers at a Klan Meeting. This is *definitely* a buzzkill, and this feeling persists for a half hour and another pint until in through the doors stumbles a bachelorette party. The star of the show, the soon-to-be wife of another man, is a fucking schoolbus; the other woman are the female equivalents of Joe Blows, and one has a clipboard and a stupid haircut and already her tangy Wal-Mart perfume has risen above the bar-musk.

These revelers are dressed for tonight's '70s show and already they're boisterous, a gang of hyenas running into a cattle paddock. The bartender, large-armed, retreats into the barback with wide eyes; you hear his knife slicing through limes and oranges, his hand dipping into a maraschino cherry jar; you listen to a peeler slicing off orange rind to garnish Old Fashioneds and Negronis. The bartender is preparing his bar out of nerves, see—he's fresh meat to this group of women. They sit at the far end of the pub and are greeted by their server while the bartender takes shelter.

Boinkable....

Ken, is that you?

It is Ken.

You ask Ken where he's been and he tells you that he's been around but just a bit tired. He suggests ordering a coffee and to pause the booze-intake for a few hours as it's not yet eight o' clock and no one will be drunk until ten-thirty. Drink some water too, Ken says.

"Whoa," you say. Buckhalter keeps his drink at mid-lift and nods.

He knows what's happening, finally sips his drink.

You tell Ken that you're not here to party and that you don't care who's drunk and who isn't.

Ken asks where exactly the fun in that is.

"I've been waiting for you," you say just as the bartender slips out from the barback, apologizes and offers you a refill. "Sorry, I'm talking to Ken."

The bartender, who you wouldn't assume has a wife or children—he's too good-looking for that—nods worriedly. "Water?" he asks.

"Please," you say. "And a coffee, too."

Ken thanks you for waiting around and notes that he's tough to get rid of.

"Right," you tell him. Buckhalter orders a shot of Jameson when the bartender comes around, who places your coffee in front of you. Buckhalter adds the shot of Jameson to your coffee. You say, "What the fuck, man," and then Buckhalter tells you to tend to Ken with intent to coax him out further from his cave. You say that being intoxicated wouldn't help, and Buckhalter tells you that being intoxicated is the *best* way to help. He orders a shot of Jameson for himself and draughts thirstily.

Now, the issue still staring you down is that you can't kill Ken in public or else face twenty-five to life with zero chance of parole. That's if you survive, of course. You have yet to determine how to kill *half* of yourself, and you left your knives and razor blades and pack of sleeping pills at home.

"How do I do it?" you ask Buckhalter.

You feel a flutter in your stomach and you know it's Ken. He wants to know what you're talking about, and you don't tell him—not immediately.

Buckhalter gazes into his Jameson with seasoned eyes, says "That's on you, man," and takes his shot. He winces, chases his Jamo with an audible gulp of water, orders a soda water with a lime wedge.

Your phone is your pacifier and you gaze at your wallpaper which is a photograph of Wifey and Boris smiling on the couch, your Happy

Place—the new generation's dinner table. You feel further fluttering in your stomach. This is Ken. You know it's Ken.

Someone says, "Nice afro."

Your immediate reply goes like this, and you curse your inebriated reflexes:

"Nice chest," you reply to the feminine voice which came from behind you. A woman from the bachelorette party is standing there. Her rack is a perky rack, by no means large, but by no means semblant of a prepubescent fat boy like Tee Aitch Oh Em Eh Ess, whose haunting voice you hear only moments after in the halls of your mind, but it's soft; delicate; reserved; nearly indecipherable.

Be better.

Taken aback this woman is at first, through her cast of makeup appears a slow but sure grin. She slaps your shoulder, expresses admiration towards your wardrobe.

"Got it from the Goodwill," you say.

You watch this stranger shiver in orgasmic repose as she says with a hand over her heart "I fucking *love* the Goodwill!"

Ken says, "Want a drink?"

She does.

THIRTY-ONE

Feel the dread and the remorse and the regret and the shame once this woman whose name you don't know accepts a drink from the bartender bought by you motherfucker—by *you.* The woman thanks you, tells you her name and you tell her yours—Don Draper would've done this as cool as a cucumber, but here you are, hot and sweaty under a blond afro with Wifey and Boris staring out at you from the depths of your mind. Soothsaying Thomas is somewhere in there, too.

Remember your hanging body.

Remember your foretold suicide; your bloated person and the man cumming in your wife not long after your death to give Boris a sibling he'd come to admire—a sibling he didn't know he wanted. This man is a man your wife loves, the man she deserves. He's everything you aren't. You're a fool who buys strange women drinks; a buffoon who can't tell a banana from a buttercup.

The woman, who's a bridesmaid, is looking at you now with glazed-over drunken eyes—possibly she's stoned. She tells you and Buckhalter that the wedding is three days away and that the ceremony will take place in Barbados with a select few attendees consisting of friends and immediate family. The bridesmaid shares with you that the bride doesn't give a shit about her second and third and fourth cousins nor her aunts and uncles of the same ilk. "Again," the bridesmaid says. "Just friends and family."

"I wish *I* got married in Barbados," you croon.

And then the bridesmaid goes, "You're *married?!"* And then she draws a finger over her index finger and goes, "Tsk tsk tsk tsk tsk tsk tsk."

Ken ripostes, "Separated."

Fucking liar, you think, and then you go, "No—"

And then Ken finishes, "Nearly divorced. It's been a while."

"A while since what?"

"Since we separated," Ken clarifies. "Going on two years."

The bridesmaid goes on to say that it's good you're out of the house and having fun. Apparently, her ex-husband, after their divorce, wasted away in his apartment for months and withered to a conservative hundred-thirty pounds and then bought a one-way ticket to an unknown location in East Asia. Nobody ever saw him again and she has yet to receive an alimony payment. Her husband was a lawyer and she wanted a piece of the pie moving forward even though she was the one who initiated the entire debacle. She went to Vegas and sucked-off a stripper and fell in love with an Elvis impersonator who she quickly discovered had an affinity for smelling tourist shoes.

Internally you war with Ken, but the guy has taken over. It's like you're looking down two long tunnels from a seat on the fabric of your brain. These tunnels are your orbital cavities. Ken's laughing and taking the bridesmaid along for the ride now; you turn to look at Buckhalter but your gaze is clung to the bridesmaid's. She's laughing—sincerely, too, it seems—and Ken asks her about her favourite '70s bands. "Disco," she says. She doesn't know shit about the '70s, just like you.

"What's yours?" she asks.

"John Wayne Gacy," Ken says.

The bridesmaid pauses, steps back from the bar and shoots Ken a pouty look. You tell Ken to stop, to get up and leave with Buckhalter.

Ken hears nothing.

"Gacy's the guy who raped and murdered all those boys, right? The pedophile who liked clowns and dressed up as one, too?"

Ken nods.

"That's hilarious!" The bridesmaid roars with laughter. "Pedophile jokes are the best!"

You think, Oh my God, and massage the bridge of your nose.

The first band takes the stage five minutes late and the house is packed and it smells like a deep fryer and spilled beer and faint on the air is the oddly refreshing waft of urinal cake. People dance and people sing and people grind on other people and you tumble drunkenly on the dance floor with Ken at the helm. You've been introduced to the rest of the bridal party, including the bride who very much looks forward to the Male Escort awaiting her at their hotel for the night.

"Maybe I'll see ya there," says the plastered bride.

Maybe not, you say, but Ken says, "Sure!" and gives the soon-to-be-wed a high-five.

Smack!

And the border separating you and Ken further blurs; you no longer feel as though you've been restrained at the end of two long tunnels as much as you feel as though simply you've lost all hope at regaining control of the ship that is you; you gaze around the packed dancefloor and see Buckhalter face-deep in a bowl of nachos at a table full of Filipino cigarette dealers, and he's encouraging you but watching closely. This is sobering, but this moment of brief clarity is only that:

Brief.

You dance; you shake your head and wiggle your bottom and shoot the dice and shoot the dice and shoot the dice again as you're encouraged to do this on repeat. You're the talk of the town—at least it feels this way—and the band just started playing Take Me Out by Frans Ferdinand, and you love it, you degenerate.

You *love* it.

You fucking *love* it, Fuckhead.

And you find yet another pint in your hand and begrudgingly you drink—you're binge-drinking now and the fog encroaches; from this point on any money spent on booze is money wasted, yet you insist on buying the bridesmaid and the bride tequila shots.

Yeah, it's that kind of night.

And you chase the José Cuervo with a salted lime. It's almost like the tequila sobers you up. For moments you swear you're walking straight and seeing clearly and that you've held a mutiny on your pirate ship and have regained control. You swear you've thrown Ken overboard as you look out into the crowd of revellers—a transient mist hovers like a sparkling cloud atop the dancefloor.

Everybody's looking at you.

"Hello," you say.

"Hello," everybody says in a unified reply. The room slowly brightens with a new day's sun. The bridesmaid stands next to you, as does the bride, and Buckhalter remains at the table with the Filipinos but he's at attention just like all the others—taut like a raging erection with two dilated urethras for eyes.

"What's happening?" you ask. Your voice is loud.

This is The Land of Whoops.

"What?" you ask. "Where are you?"

You can't see me, I reply. I said, this is The Land of Whoops.

You think, *Fucking tequila,* and shake your head. It gets you every time.

"Who's talking?" you ask.

I am, I say.

"Who are you?" you ask.

I'm God, I say, and then you reply, "No way," you say. "That's bullshit. There is no God." And then I say, Yeah, wouldn't that be nice. I wish I had nothing to do with humanity just like you wish you were in control of your own life. This is all part of a grander plan, see.

I remind you that this is The Land of Whoops, and that we all show up here from time-to-time. I once spent an entire day here, on the Seventh Day after I created the universe. I sat here and thought *Whoops* all day long and I called the Seventh day, Sabbath, and then I decided that alcohol wasn't for me. I get too creative when I drink.

Uncontrollably creative, really.

You stand idle while I speak, just like all the others. You're no different than them, caught in regret and countless *whoopsies* while God talks to them, sobering them up. I'm talking to everybody all at once, but only you can hear what I'm saying to you; Buckhalter hears only what I say to him; the bridesmaid and the bride hear only what I say to them, and so on.

I want you to know that you look like an asshole in your blond afro and that with a quick Facebook search the bridesmaid knows you're not separated; she knows you have a kid, and critically, she doesn't know about Ken. She thinks Ken is you, just like your wife thinks you are you, so I ask you this:

Who are you?

This is what hangovers are for.

You sleep poorly, waking before the sun has but an inkling of motivation to deal with another day and your mouth is a swamp and an orchestra is playing a percussion symphony in your cranial cavity. You feel your pulse in your eyes. You're at Buckhalter's house and your head is itchy from wearing that blond afro to sleep. There's no way Buckhalter's awake.

You peel from the leather sofa as though you've been rolled in Elmer's White Glue and tumble into the kitchen where you fill a glass with cold water. Drink it; feel your stomach turn; your head spinning on axis; you're on a fast-moving carousel and you're a young kid who's ate too many corndogs. You'll vomit soon and taste them all over again. Enjoy. While you're vomiting you can think about Ken and how far away he's gone. He's nowhere near you, now.

He's too smart to deal with hangovers.

This is on you.

THIRTY-TWO

This one is on you.

This on is *all* on you.

What were you thinking? How do you kill half of yourself, and what makes you think that getting drunk is the way to do it? There are too many factors when getting drunk; too many things can go wrong—especially when you're trying to kill somebody and get away with it. They could make a Netflix Documentary about you, Fuckhead.

You survive your hangover and you're mighty glad to discard your blond afro in the nearest public garbage bin whereas you keep the button-up and bellbottoms because they'd make a good Halloween costume and could serve you well should you and Wifey ever decide to open a Disco.

Home; fried eggs; bacon; a scaling hot bath to sweat out maximum alcohol and the washroom smells like run-off liquor trapped for days beneath the rolls of a double chin. You nap before noon; wake up feeling, to your delight, not horrible, but you have yet to check your cell phone which has gone unlooked-at it in a long while—and by *long-while,* I mean damn-near an entire day.

It sits ominously on the kitchen counter, a totem of the badgering world. If you were to bet an over/under of twenty text messages, you'd take the over, and they'd be from both your wife and mother sprinkled among upwards of five missed calls. What were you doing? Is everything okay? Do you be honest, or do you lie?

You elect honesty, check your phone.

Ten texts, eight missed calls. You're not that important, Fuckhead; you're not worthy of upwards of twenty unread texts.

"Wife," you say to your love as she answers the phone, and then you feel the ice on your her voice as it slithers outta the cell phone's speaker. It turns yours nipples to glass. "I went out with my best friend, Buckhalter, and we soused through the night."

"You were too busy carousing to reply to any of my messages?"

You tell Wifey that you forgot your phone. Afterall, this is the truth. Your phone wouldn't have fit the bellbottoms's pocket anyways. She more or less backs off after this, tells you that the plan is to be home tomorrow evening by five—your mother-in-law *did* plan a lunch, and it's a considerable one.

Imagine poor attempts at Food Network recipes, the mimosas and a cheese dip which has not had the white wine cooked out of it. Worst case scenario is that she tries a recipe she saw on Pinterest.

"Right," you say. "Love you, Wife."

"Love you too, Husband."

And the connection is split and again you're on your own and you have last night to think about—Ken is too far away to point out any laughable memories from the night prior aside from yourself as a person, totally unrecognizable to who you've always known yourself to be. What a shame.

Dwell in the regret and never forget this sensation; recall Tee Aitch Oh Em Eh Ess and his foreboding words and the portentous dream he provided you.

See your bloated corpse dangling by the throat; see your wife take the hand of a man who deserves a woman like her in marriage; see Boris and his sister and a future ahead of him that you can very well miss should you traipse too far into Ken's malevolent domain—

But you did this *for* your family—your goal was to coax Ken out of his cage to kill him, but he fooled you; the rascal pulled the wool over your eyes and seized complete control and woulda shtuck a bridesmaid if it weren't for your arrival in The Land of Whoops.

You wince as your turn down the television, ultimately turning it off because your headaches rears its ugly head and suddenly the room seems too bright. You close your eyes for a few moments; nausea is afoot and your light breakfast isn't sitting well in your stomach nor has what you've done yet settled in your mind. These are things you must deal with, and again, thank God for The Land of Whoops.

"Come out, Ken," you say. "Come out come out wherever you are!"

Crickets sound in reply.

"I just wanna talk."

Crickets again.

"Ken, I want you to know that you're not going to bring me down," you say. "You'll never gain control ever again and if you ever come near me or my family I will put an end to us. There will be no more."

Distant laughs.

Ken says from so far away it's near impossible to perceive, but it's there, "I am eternal."

You reply, "So long as I let you," and the remainder of the day is slept away, but at least you finish your latest watch of Mad Men.

THIRTY-THREE

You're virgin-new come morning and the sun is shining and you can see the accumulation of the weekend's dust gathered upon all flat surfaces and your laundry heaps at the bases of all three baskets and you've yet to unload the dishwasher and then load it and after that you could probably cook yourself a nice lunch—maybe a chicken salad sandwich or something like that. But maybe just leftover pizza—it all comes down to how productive you feel once the afternoon rolls in, the shallows of Wifey and Boris's return. Dare it be considered that you look forward to their return, thoughts of Thursday and looking forward to alone-time feeling about as distant as Jupiter's Titan.

Up first is the dishwasher, both unloaded and loaded and activated. Chances are good that you'll unload it before Wifey gets back, to delight her by ridding the sink and counter of what clutter might remain. You put in a load of laundry, you dust the kitchen table and the coffee table and the television screen and open the window to air the place out because your home smells heavily of cleaning detergent and you didn't even commit a murder.

Bullshit bullshit, you pop the washed laundry in the dryer and start a second load. Right on. You whip-up a nutritious lunch and eat an amount that's a far shot from nutritious; you add your dirty dishes to the dishwasher, activate it. The dishwasher whirs, the dryer stops, and so on.

You go for a walk to account for the fresh air you missed yesterday. The early summer air is invigorating. You're invigorated; prepared to welcome your family home; prepared to deal hugs and a pair of matching smooches. Maybe you'll even cook them a second lunch, or maybe they'll be fine with leftover pizza, who knows—you still got about three-quarters of a whole pie cooling in your refrigerator and pizza is the last thing you feel like eating. Probably it'll go stale in there, but Boris surely hasn't ate, you think; and Wifey's likely forced her way through a couple servings of an extremely bland *something*, you think further. Maybe pizza would do them well—maybe.

It's either she'll be hungry or she won't—dealer's choice, you think. She and Boris will be home before you know it and you won't have days like this again for the foreseeable future. You tell yourself that you'll enjoy this last little while to the fullest and that once you get the house up to Wifey's cleanliness standards you'll retire to the sofa, and though disgusted by alcohol given your latest—and probably final—foray into nightlife, you'll crack a beer because it just seems *right.*

You put the dustpan down and the beer tastes good and by no means does it disgust you so you have two more—you aren't even thirsty, but the beer tastes good. It's deserved. It's bubbly. It's malty. It hit the motherfuckin' spot, man, and in these shallows of a returning life dare you consider this delicate twinge in your stomach similar to the thaumaturgical sensation you no longer feel at the first sign of Christmas—that buzz found in your youth which no longer accompanies the year's first snowfall now replaced by the dread of supping on a scandalously overcooked turkey, allergies, feeble attempts at goose dinners and crowded living rooms and the smell of burnt coffee; now you feel like a magnet and your polar-pair is nearby; there's a tug in the center of your chest as though you've got a hook in there pulling you towards better things—things you've missed this past weekend, this lifetime; what returns is all the colour in an otherwise monochromatic world and you're particularly fond of daisies and roses and daffodils and lilies and chrysanthemums; and it's not long before you're pulled from the seat of your sofa to the window, where you overlook your quaint street in anticipation of Boris and your wife.

Ah, there they are—there they are in your in-laws' white Honda Pilot—

No, wait: that was just your frugal neighbour's friends or something. You try to return to the couch but it rejects you like there's an invisible springboard there so you do another go-around of your house to ensure things have been returned to their places and that the place is, all-in-all, clean—you'd hate to see Wifey immediately change into her favourite pair of polyester shorts and baggy black tee just to start scrubbing surfaces you'd recently scrubbed, to place cleaned dishes in for another round in the Whirlpool while criticizing your latest attempt at laundry—

Ah, speaking of which:

You remove the dried stuff from the dryer and add the wet stuff from the washer to the dryer.

Activate.

Carry the dried stuff to the sofa, begin sorting panties from boxers and Boris's garb from both yours and your wife's. You get through half of the basket before you hear distant Goodbyes and a couple shutting doors, and then your front door swings open and the first word you hear is

"Daddy!" and pattering feet despite the bottom of his runners being caked in rural muck.

Fuck the rug.

Your little man hugs tight for being a little guy—you even feel an urge to push him away so you can draw breath, but you don't. Boris smells like squirrels and smoke and you'd happily let him choke you to death if that were the cost of a hug as good as this.

You ask Wifey what her mother made for lunch.

"A meat platter," your wife says, then farts. You give her a kiss; she gives you a kiss—blah blah blah. Boris wants one, too. His wish is your command.

Light conversation lasts as long as is fitting before Wifey says to Boris that she's heading for a bath. Boris, excitedly, asks to tag along. Your wife accepts him, tells you to unload the dishwasher. It recently stopped. You oblige her, the dishwasher is empty before long and you grab another beer. This will be your last of the day and you put on the first sporting event that shows up on the TV Guide, an MLB game and you can tolerate baseball, but you're not watching the game—no. What your paying attention to is this:

The laughter echoing from the bathroom and down the hall, in instances the laughter so powerful you think Boris is choking or crying but Wifey's laughing too so that nullifies any chance of trouble and is something you can never quite get enough of. You may as well have your eyes shut because all you see are smiles despite the game being in the bottom of the ninth with the bases loaded, two outs and a full count with the winning run at Third and cheating towards Homeplate; you listen to splashes outta the tub-shallows and the indecipherable jabberings of the weekend and something about watching a mommy deer with her babies grazing by the woodpile, and then there's further laughter, and further laughter, and you put your beer down and turn off the TV in favour for the noise of your quiet house which at last has been refilled with home.

You listen to Heaven.

THIRTY-FOUR

Sometimes the emotion is too much.

Consider this:

The cheeseburger of your wildest dreams is in front of you and it will never cool down. This cheeseburger is immensely hot—it has the heat of the charcoals over which it was cooked. It would be sacrilege to allow this cheeseburger to go uneaten, therefore you take a bite and burn yourself.

This is what it's like raising a toddler who's aware of the love they have for you. You simply can't let them waste away because these are moments you have and then don't have and will never have *ever* again. Experience them or don't—burn yourself or don't. You live with what you've seized and what you've missed.

Five days a week, on workdays, you wonder throughout which milestones you're missing. You came home at the beginning of the month and Boris asked you for five dollars. "Why?" you asked. "For nuggets," Boris said. "I wuv nuggets."

He took his first steps, though a year ago, on a Tuesday. You were watering the boulevard marigolds during rush-hour while cursing the geriatric blue-hair who cut you off three blocks earlier.

He made his first friend on a Wednesday. You were still working.

Boris is becoming a man by the minute and it kills you to know you're not around for upwards of forty hours a week.

You're resting your head on the steering wheel when Clyde and Brianne return from their Whopper-run. Clyde asks what's wrong.

"You wouldn't get it," you reply.

It was less than two years ago when you were in the same boat and you're not sure if that ignorance was a blessing or a curse.

Boris turned two, by the way—can't say I'm sure you're aware of that given your full-time job and reasonable exhaustion. He started using the potty around Christmas and finds it hilarious when either you or your wife snap pictures of his feces and subsequently text these photographs to his grandparents—your wife did this after his first trip to the john and he thought this was the funniest thing in all human history. He wants pictures taken of his poop every time he poops, and sometimes he'll try to poop twice. His pediatrician told you to watch out for prolapses and hemorrhoids and noted that Tuck's Anal

Ointment is fine should trouble ever arise, barring the case of prolapse, which terrifies you even though it's still pretty hilarious. A prolapse would require a hospital, and quickly.

Emotion can be an issue.

It *will* be an issue.

And it is, right now, an issue.

Wifey cooked a breakfast skillet and it sits steaming in the center of the kitchen table. Boris is staring at it, entertained by the steam which rises in tendrils to the ceiling. "Your plate's cooling down in the fridge," says your wife to your son. "Drink your orange juice, breakfast'll be up before you know it."

"Okay!" says Boris. "Wawn my tablet, though."

Right. You stand to harvest your little man's morningly helping of drugs. He thanks you. You tell him that he's welcome to pester you and order you around, even if his tablet isn't ten feet away in his favourite sitting corner, sticky with old ketchup and grimy toddler fingerprints, the screen scratched because one time he took a fork to it in an attempt to use it as a stylus. You sit, help yourself to a serving of the breakfast skillet and further steam escapes from the depths of the cast iron. It's like someone set off a smoke-bomb. You add a squirt of ketchup and a healthy dose of Tabasco, and then your wife slides Boris his plate and sits next to you with a dish of her own.

Boris's feet patter the bottom of the table, sending ripples across the surface of your coffee and your water, a slow heartbeat and hypnotizes you and you fall into the muted yet percussive beat—he's wearing socks, so the noise is nearly inaudible; you feel it more than you hear it, like walloping subwoofers at the far end of the street. The beat draws your gaze to Boris whose face keeps oblivious to your intrusive stares. His kicking of the table's bottom persists, his cheeks still filled with baby fat and his hair yet wonderfully unkempt—you'd reach across the table and give him a hug and a kiss if doing so didn't mean disrupting him from sitting quietly in anticipation of a breakfast he'll surely wolf-down; you'd reach across the table and give him all the love you can give a child if only this were the slightest bit possible….

You say, "Love you, kiddo."

And Boris's reply is this:

"I'm eating!"

You bloat further with love indescribable.

There's no other way to put it, but whenever you're able to focus on it, there's such copious amounts of love it hurts.

THIRTY-FIVE

When people who have been parents longer than you tell you that Time flies, these are the times they're talking about.

Looking back, you can already see it. From the day you and Wifey came home with Boris until his first birthday, you simply cannot remember what you did. What do you do with a baby? Where do you put it? Did you really change upwards of ten diapers a day? Were your wife's boobs as voluptuous as your memory tells you they were, or was such a magnificent rack just your imagination?

Zero to one is kept beneath a haze, and one to two is nearly the same. A one-year-old was surely crawling, getting into things and learning the definition of the two-letter word meaning either:

FUCKINGPUTTHATFUCKINGTHINGDOWN!

or

EATTHESHITYOUHAVEONYOURFUCKINGPLATE!

No, in other words.

You know a two-year-old is walking and amid the challenges of potty training and only soiling themselves occasionally. Boris is developing like a weed at this age; it's nearly every day he learns a new skill or copies a word you've never heard him say before. These days you're forced to mind your language because you don't want a toddler muttering nasties at preschool, which is already less than two years away.

I'm going to stop listing off things you know because it's useless simply refreshing your mind. Here's a brilliant piece of advice, told forthrightly, that not only parents but every living human could benefit from knowing:

Slow down. Time flies because of an undying hunger for more while Heaven is the present. Heaven isn't a reward you work towards but a reward you already have so long as you're aware you see it. Do the right thing to the best of your ability and remain focused. This is Heaven, that's it. Be in it. I'm warning you, Fuckhead, that two to three will fly by at a rate so mind-boggling and indelible that you'll look back through your phone's Gallery and see pictures and think, No, that never happened, or, Boris could never have looked like that….

You'll long for the infantile laughs you recorded on your phone nigh months ago and try (and fail) to reach through your phone's LED screen to pat a taught belly and diaper so full it looks like it's been filled with porridge and wads of brown sugar. One day you'll gather Boris from his crib and his chubby cheeks will be gone as though he'd dreamed them away—somewhere in the past you will have blinked, forgot how *perfect* they were in a mere sliver in Time—and you'll cry. I might as well be honest, right?

Not only fall into *today*, but fall into this very *second.*

It's gone already. See how fast Time moves? That second has been spent and you'll never have it again.

Time flies, they say.

They're not lying.

THIRTY-SIX

You took my advice. I'm proud of you—congratulations. I clap upon my holy throne and lightning flashes and thunder sounds and small creatures hide in their burrows, their nests. Pussies hide in their houses and parents tell their children, "Nope, we're not going to go splash in the puddles because you'll get dirty and catch a cold."

These parents are both liars and assholes and also an array of thousands of adjectives which suit their preferences, the sluggards; the sloths; the couch potatoes and the laggards and the layabouts. Pick up your feet, deadbeat, and tend to your children who are not trying to bother you but are simply curious, woolgatherer. Set your book down, or your cell phone; turn off the television and whatever else keeps you idle and tend to your children in the times where they wonder and allow them to flourish as children are meant to do less you wish to raise someone as inactive as yourself.

Raindrops pepper your house in a way you haven't experienced in years. It sounds like a group of vandals stand on the curb interspersing your house with paintballs. Boris is pushed back into his corner of the sofa, his eyes wide and intent at the windows. He notes that it's raining.

"It is," you say.

"Wawn go outside."

You ask Boris if he's sure, and of course he replies in the affirmative. "Like George and Peppa Pig," he says. "Wawn jump in muddy puddles."

Your reply is this:

"Do you see how the trees are nearly bent parallel to the ground?"

"Uh-huh."

And you go on, "Maybe we can go outside when there's no threat of being whisked away to the Land of Oz."

"I like Oz," Boris says.

"Excellent movie," you tell him.

"But I wawn go outside."

It's now when you feel it in the pit of your stomach, not a tickle as much as it's a twinge. This is where your desires and what's best for Boris intersect and rarely do these roads run in the same direction—oftentimes they criss-cross and sometimes accidents happen. Your wife will be home from work in an hour and it's this hour which drags longer than a bad joke to which you know the punchline. This is a decent way to pass the time but you already know the outcome: You'll gear Boris up, you'll head outside and once he feels the cold wind and the sideways raindrops slapping his unseasoned cheeks he will cry and beg to come inside.

You say "It'll be very cold, okay?"

Boris shoots up from his seat and proclaims "Okay!" He runs to the front door where he grabs his pair of yellow rainboots. You remind him that he needs pants. He follows you to his bedroom where he succeeds at putting them on himself. Finding success only took five minutes and it seems the rain has calmed in that span, or maybe this is just your imagination getting the better of you. Probably it is. You still hear the wind howling ghoulishly through the fan in your bathroom and the hood vents above the gas range; it sounds like a hundred Keebler Elves are doing a dance on your roof and you think, Fuck, Christmas is four months away—

You slap your cheek just hard enough to remind yourself that Boris is critical and that loathing the approaching yuletide season will only instill you in a misery no one but other husbands and fathers and a thin selection of moms and wives and various singles understand, especially if they don't celebrate the Holiday.

Hear the sleighbells ringalin' jing-ting-a-tingalin' toooooo.

"Okay, hurry up," you say to your boy, ushering him to the front door. He waddles down the hallway, pauses at the closet in waiting for the application of his slicker. It's so long it nearly touches the tops of his boots. You ask him if he's ready to rock.

"Uh-huh!" he says excitedly, stationed at the door. You open it. The wind peels off his hood. "Whoa!" he says, struggling to reapply what's been blown off. You give him a helping hand and he starts down the path to the sidewalk. The sidewalk is now a lake.

Boris jumps it in.

Fortunately: his slicker; his boots; a pair of waterproof mitts. His hood's already been blown off but he's willingly letting the storm have its way with him. He's smiling, you can see his ivory baby teeth as his cheeks are pulled up to his earlobes. A gust of wind nearly pushes him over but he endures, mutters another "Whoa," once regaining his balance, deep up to his boot-tops in the puddle in the bowed sidewalk. Waves roll over it like it's an ocean for ants and other small things. It'll make a nice lake on a sunny day, you think. Until it evaporates, or a dog shits in it. Then again, what's so different between that and a regular lake?

These are the things you wonder while your child has fun.

"Daddy come!"

"No way," you say. The wind—thank *Me*—grabs hold of your words and takes them with it at forty miles-per-hour and they turn to nothing by the time they reach the end of the street.

Boris repeats what he said. You hear him loud and clear.

You show him your shoes. They're not rainboots. You're also wearing old black sweatpants that you've owned for a decade. They're disposable sweatpants.

Boris repeats what he said. You still hear him loud and clear.

"Next time," you say.

The wind does what's best for Boris. Your words don't make it to him. He stands expectantly, his smile enduring through cold and these truly adverse conditions, his cheeks reddened by the chill and appearing as plump and as pinchable as anything you've ever seen before.

"Want some hot chocolate?" you ask. This is more so a bribe. You're cold; you're ready to go inside. Your dick is shrivelled to the point of it being considered a dink. It hurts a little bit.

Boris doesn't hear you, and it's when you see the corners of his cheeks descend to his chin that you take a step towards him and his cheeks quickly twitch back up to their upright and ready positions. Boris shouts "YAY!" and you can't help but smile yourself. He bobs up and down in joy, jumping in the puddle and splashing his slicker.

Your socks are wet anyways, and Chuck Taylors have a thing for enduring hardships. You wear them in the winter, too—Chuck Taylors are the perfect shoe. Far from anything water-resistant, though….

The rainwater bites your feet but once one foot is entirely submerged the other naturally follows but you hardly feel anything at all aside from the warmth of the moment.

You jump in muddy puddles with your child and then the moment is done before you know it, an ephemeral blink now among the billions which came before.

THIRTY-SEVEN

Boris naps on the couch beneath a large afghan as you sip a rum-imbued hot apple cider. The rain hasn't slowed and thunder rolls on occasion and your clothes and your son's were tossed into the washing machine. They stew with bath towels and underwear.

If this isn't comfort, what is?

Wifey got home twenty minutes ago, she sits in a bubble bath with her book and a glass of pinot noir; she told you she'll make chicken pot pie for supper, a recipe handed down to her from her grandmother. You liked her grandmother. Tomorrow is Sunday.

Again, if this isn't comfort, what is?

THIRTY-EIGHT

Tomorrow is today. Sunday. The rain has stopped and last night you dreamed of nothing because you lived your dreams yesterday. There was nothing left to dream about; you did what you were supposed to do and this morning you feel particularly dainty—yes, dainty. There are no problems with this. Qualms be gone. Dainty is good. Dainty is for everybody. The day is new and Boris sleeps-in—he sleeps to an hour late enough for you to cook yourself and Wifey a nice breakfast.

Monday seems as though it's a week away despite the looming need to clock in at work in less than twenty-four hours. This looms, yes, but by no means is your mood affected. It will be a good day, you're sure of it. You could be due to report for military service tomorrow and you'd go smiling; you could die in that war knowing that you had what was possibly the best day of your life yesterday, and then a Sunday to drink it all in.

What was it that made it so fantastic, though? There was absolutely nothing comfortable about it until you and your boy were inside, napping on the sofa and warming up as one, your wife returning from work and heading to the bath soon after knowing she'd be undisturbed. And then chicken pot pie, an early bedtime and rising the next day—today—with the sun. Now: eggs benedict.

But before then, on the sidewalk with Boris you were numb to the unsatisfying; oblivious to splashing ankle-deep in puddles and jumping up and down like you were a boy again, Boris watching, learning. It was that constant look on his face that really got you, his eyes like golf balls, his cheeks and forehead taut in suspended excitement. *I can have fun just like Dad,* Boris thought—you're sure of it.

This is how you want him to feel.

You're proud of yourself and you've earned this feeling of contentedness; you deserve a poached egg atop prosciutto and toasted english muffin all beneath a blood-clotting serving of butter and egg-yolk and lemon and salt and pepper.

You cook.

You and Wifey eat.

Meanwhile:

Another force stirs in your abode, unnoticed. You're used to Ken because he's a part of you, yet still he watches from places that are yours and he twiddles his thumbs with menacing intent. He'll rear his head when you least expect it and his arrival will come without recognition.

He waits.

THIRTY-NINE

This is a slow descent into madness.

He wasn't meant for this.

Fatherhood, that is.

But why? Afterall, you love it and you're at the helm—you're the leader or your life, the captain of your ship and you've never been happier. Thoughts of the years before Boris, years of tomfoolery and tomfuckery and cockjackery and shenanigans alike are distant beyond recollection, and this is for the better—for one of you, that is. The other is hungered, wanting.

Neglected.

Vociferous. Lonely.

He calls you by name but his voice falls on your ears with the weight of a seed caught in a spring breeze—you're preoccupied with pushing-duty. Boris is on a swing set and has yet to familiarize himself with the act of pumping. Days later, while shaving, Ken shows himself in the mirror as you draw the razor over your stubbled cheek. He wants you to shave your pubes, but you're too smart for that—there's no point in doing that less you have a desire to impress your wife with a groomed bush, but then again, you don't want your wife looking at your dick anyways. That always goes over on the odder side of events: receiving a blowjob but your wife backing off to just stare at your pecker as though she were expecting it to be a pepperette, then going on to munch on it lengthwise like a buttered corncob. Surely it's salty. All it's missing is a few cracks of fresh black pepper.

Ken withers. His next attempt at influencing you comes over dinner. You made lasagna and it turned out great. You see no possible way for improvement; the mozzarella is crisped around the edges and is browned in some spots and humped which will pop when sliced; it held its form when served like a good piece of cake, and it steamed, and the ricotta and cottage cheeses in the center layer rounds it all out with an element of cream. You use garlic toast to mop up what juices remain and wash it all down with a glass of shiraz. See, what Ken wanted you to do here was to invite an old friend over—Muriel—who's in town for the weekend. The text would've pled, **Come have dinner with me and the family!** but your intentions—Ken's intentions—deep down were to squeak yourself into someone else's life for future flirting potential. You didn't text Muriel. You just enjoyed your lasagna and received many compliments, and then watched Muriel's Instagram intently to see what she was up to in town. Turns out that she went for drinks with Buckhalter, and then Buckhalter sent you a message saying that you were missing out.

You had your doubts.

And today you sit in your backyard looking at a large cardboard box and two larger ones which contain the elements to a play-structure for Boris and nobody else. It's got two slides, one that goes down straight and one that you'd formerly refer to as a *twirly* slide. There's a small set of monkey bars which go five rungs, and a bridge and a rock-climbing wall fit with a rope to repel—something Boris will probably lose a tooth on, you figure, but the thing was 50% off during the START OF SUMMER SALE at the local hardware store and you'd think yourself an idiot for letting such a deal pass. It also has two swings and a detachable/attachable baby adapter, the thing that looks like a diaper. There's a tunnel, too, and a sandbox beneath all of it. You hope to erect it by suppertime. Tacos, the wife tells you.

There's nothing wrong with tacos.

And so you build.

Planks line-up with planks and you drive screws through the precut holes and you've got a platform before you know it. You build-out toward another platform and then you attach the big plastic slide. It's orange and it bows when you take a test slide all on your own. You build and build and assemble until the thing's built and then step back from it, three hours later, and you give yourself a pat on the back. Boris will love it, you think, and just then he and your wife come searing outta the patio door.

"Wow," says Boris, in awe. "Wow," he says again, enthralled in stupefaction, and then repeats himself for a third time in case nobody heard the first two. He stands beside you, his back straight and his hands at his side. Wifey tells him to say thanks.

"Tanks," Boris says, and then starts to your creation in a slow wobble—his hands hardly sway upon his approach. He may as well be walking uphill with his hands in his pockets.

Your wife takes over while you head in to shower, but you do this once having watched the kiddo frolic about on his new toy for a while. If Boris's affection towards his other toys are any sign of how long the excitement towards this $750 contraption will last, he'll be bored with it by next weekend.

So, you're in the shower and soaping your ass with your wife's loofa and stuff and then you wash your hair, moisturize your face. Probably you can get away with another shave, as while washing your mug it's as though your cheeks are two Brillo Pads. You think, Very few things in life are better than a shower beer. You're drinking a Heineken right from its smooth green bottle and it beads with condensation. The water running down the drain is grey with dirt. Building that play-structure was hard work. You deserve tacos, hell yeah you do. You deserve a *dozen* tacos.

Sparkling clean and gleaming you exit the shower, dry yourself and head to the sink to warm your razor and to apply a shave oil and then shave cream in sequence—soon enough you'll be Heineken-bottle-smooth—and then you'll smack your cheeks and throat with palms full of Taylor of Old Bond Street aftershave. You'll smell great and the sting will be invigorating and nothing less. You wipe clean a section of the mirror and Ken is waiting there.

You tell him to go away.

He refuses.

You ask why.

He says there's no escape and that he's always around.

You say, "Well that sounds like a spectacular waste of time."

And then Ken says that there's more to life than being around your family. He says that *this* is truly wasting time.

You disagree, and Ken disagrees with you, so…yeah. There's that.

A standoff, and you're nowhere near as cool as The Outlaw Josie Wales.

You'd punch Ken in the face if it didn't mean shattering your mirror. His smug grin would be better off in shambles on the bathroom floor. Your fists are stones.

Ken takes the first shot. He says that you regret everything about this—about fatherhood.

You don't. You say No.

Then explain why you almost took that job with Gyles and Kilgore, Ken says. Why did you almost fuck that bridesmaid from the bachelorette party?

I wasn't gonna fuck her, you tell Ken. "Buckhalter just wanted to take me out for a night on the town."

No, Ken says. Buckhalter wanted to take you out so you could get a shot at me. You got black-out drunk instead. That was me, you know. You just overdid it by a hair and if you had two less shots your cock woulda been wet with extra-marital cunt.

Recall: The Land of Whoops.

Recall: waking up the next morning with a monumental hangover.

You wonder if you could take a shot now. How do I kill half of myself? you wonder. The razor blades are in the medicine chest, you could try slitting just one wrist, but by doing that you'd miss out on Tacos for dinner and that's far from appealing. You peer into the place where all the pills are kept and you contemplate a handful of melatonin, you'd take it and then head into the kitchen and set the coffee pot with the strongest beans you got and drink it all in a hasty chug, possibly adding a few ice cubes so it would go down with minimal burn. Then again, you're no pharmacist and you have no clue how much melatonin you'd need to do the job.

If you could end it all right now, you'd take the shot.

You just don't know. That's all. You don't know what to do.

All you can do is walk away shaved and soaped and cleaned, glimmering, and start the tacos.

You watch your perfect wife and your perfect son play while you assemble supper.

You beam; Ken wilts.

FORTY

This is an ending or a beginning—maybe both.

You reach a tipping-point when Wifey approaches you and says, "My friend, the one I've known all my life—the one from roughly thirty chapters ago—wants to go do a bunch of drugs and dance like slutty pixies at a rave in California."

Being a man of frugality, you ask, "And where do you think we'll get the money for that?"

"My parents," says your wife, and then she flourishes a plane ticket and notes that they gave her $1500 spending money as an advance on their Estate. It's not like they're going to die anytime soon as much as it is they spoil their daughter, and sometimes some children have parents like that. Must be nice.

And this is where things get complicated.

See, you're imperfect; you've fucked up and you've acted on impulse and you've stepped on toes including your wife's but she loves you for reasons you'll never comprehend because you're a Fuckhead and Fuckheads can't keep good things.

So, Fuckhead, your wife's going on a lady-trip with a group of spiteful degenerate thirty-year-old exhibitionist coots and you can't do a single thing about it — well you can always tell her "BITCH! You're staying home," but that wouldn't go over too well for your reputation — so you proceed to say, "Well, shit," and you slouch into your lounger. Boris sits on the sofa flipping idly through a Where's Waldo?

Your wife tells you that there's nothing to worry about.

You do everything in your power to believe her but your power is minimal in comparison to your raging anxiety. "When do you leave?" you ask.

"This weekend."

How fitting. How appropriate. How sudden. Right when we begin running out of things to talk about.

Ken? you ask.

Ken appears.

"Daddy?" says Boris.

You forget about Ken, though temporarily. Boris wipes clean any malicious thoughts from the tarnished canvas that is you and you head to your boy and inquire what's the matter. All he wants is a hug. It turns out that's all you wanted as well. Though small, the size of a toddler, Boris fills your arms and your heart alike and ages pass while in this three-second embrace. He says that he loves you. You say that you love him, too.

A boys' weekend approaches, and it begins like this:

"Bye-bye my baby boy," your wife says.

Boris says, "Bye-bye mommy!" and gives her a peck on the cheek.

"Bye, love," you say. Wifey tells you not to worry and plants one on your lips. It's a bitter kiss as by no means are you comfortable with what looms as her friends await her on the opposite side of Boarding. One of them pretends to stroke a large cock while another simulates a blowjob on the straw in a Burger King cup and another one dry-humps the shit out of the last one.

Remember, this book isn't all about sex.

Wifey leaves.

C'est la vie.

You drive home, get home. Right about now, you figure, your wife is lifting off in an airplane on a trip that will test your mental fortitude as much as it'll test your wife's loyalty. Probably more so your mental fortitude, you think, as you're atremble when you pull into your driveway. Your fingers wish not to stop wiggling; your hand prefers constant vibration versus anything semblant of rest and your feet tap as though you're Neil Pert cranking out a new Rush tune. How the hell are you going to last two days on your own with Boris—your *offspring*—while kept in a cloud of unknowingness? How will you focus? How will this work?

I'm here to help.

That wasn't me. That was Ken.

No, you say.

Yes, Ken says. I'm here, he says again.

"Go away," you say.

Boris looks at you in the rear-view mirror. "Daddy what you say?"

"Nothing," you answer. "Just talking to myself." And you're right. That's exactly what you're doing. You know that your mother is available to do some babysitting—she doesn't do that nearly enough and she's always on your case about it. Buckhalter's surely got some free time—he doesn't spend too much time with his family and it seems as though he prefers *not* spending time with his family. This is a way to get your mind off things: a little bit of devilry all for yourself.

But Boris, who ogles you from his car seat, asks to go inside to watch School of Rock, by far your favourite movie of all time. Jack Black is The Man, despite he and his students saying the same about Joan Cusack's Miss Rosalie Mullins. "Want to order some pizza?" you ask.

Boris does.

This is how you spend your night, but still: you're alive with freneticism and you sleep not a blink, as live as a live wire on your sofa while watching The Lord of the Rings episode One *and* Two. You don't eat the pizza because the juices in your stomach bubble like instigated water in a stovetop kettle. Your eyes are heavy around five in the morning and this is when Boris begins to roll around in his crib. Fatherhood persists through anxiety and Boris has yet to familiarize himself with anxiety. You tell yourself, while sure at this hour in a faraway place Wifey is tempted by noxious substances and spontaneous sexual relations, that you'll make it through; that fatherhood is more than being a dad but also a good man to your woman. A splash of cool water on your face helps. Feel the nip on your flesh, your breath hitching in your throat. You look in the mirror.

He's there.

Ken.

"You," you say.

Ken says that he's just looking out for you.

You tell him that he's not helping—

"But I'm trying," Ken pleads, and quickly. He says that he doesn't want you taken advantage of—that you, too, deserve a getaway when Wifey gets back. Maybe Thailand, he suggests. A Thai vacation is still relatively cheap. Less than a couple grand, upon a blasé googling. But you're scared of flying.

Maybe not, you think, closing your phone. No Thai holidays any time soon.

Ken still looks at you, though. He retreats into the mirror with a half-smile on his face. He knows. He knows the temptation won't go away—the jealously and the envy and the uncertainty and immense distance between you and Wifey.

Boris cries. A new day soon begins and you figure that seven's a decent time to put the coffee on despite not quite feeling like a cup of joe. If you slept at all, sure—yeah, a coffee would be nice.

You didn't sleep for a second.

Boris slept for ten hours.

It'll be a day, you figure.

Oh yes. It'll be a day. A full day.

Hours pass like a toy boat through an ocean of solidifying corn syrup, morning shadows lethargically retreating to their sources and expanding again post-noon in opposing direction to their morningly paths. You feel no more awake than you did when you hoisted your son from his crib as the day approaches lunch. Broccoli should do—some broccoli and salt and a few slices of cheddar cheese. Boris ate heavy for breakfast, to your delight, therefore lunch, as is reasonable, will be light.

Boris eats it, smiling; it's as though he knows something's up with you. What an inquisitive guy, you think. He asks for a slice of leftover pizza. You oblige him and turn in for a nap around 2:00 and rise shy of 3:00. Yeah, Boris scribbled on the TV stand and the coffee table and spilled his water on the sofa, but hey: you napped. You're alive again, and you'll turn in for the night inside seven hours. Seven hours to go and you'll rise tomorrow when everything returns to normal save your wife stepping off the airplane with venereal diseases and/or tales of sexual escapades—

Shut up, Ken.

He shakes his head.

No, really.

Ken says that he won't stop; that he's doing what's best for you. Just think about what you're going to do when Wifey gets back, he tells you as Boris sits in his corner fiddling with his tablet.

"No."

Boris looks at you, confused.

"Not talking to you, kiddo," you say.

"Okay!" the little man pips.

And the day passes. You find sleep like your feet find the floor each morning and you don't want this sleep to pass; you want to dwell in it until you can rise and turn off your brain for a while, to breathe fresh air in a place where Ken can't find you because he's tuckered you so. You dream of nothing, and you wake refreshed, rolling over to face the window.

Your wife is there. She looks as she's always looked and not the slightest bit different. She sleeps. You pinch yourself. This isn't a dream.

Wake her up.

"Fuck off," you say. Wifey twitches; you cover your mouth and then tell Ken to fuck off in a way he'd understand.

This is how you do it:

You look at Wifey and call yourself an asshole for thinking that such horrible events, such occurrences, such erroneous possibilities were possible. You touch your wife's shoulder and give a light squeeze and peck her on the cheek. "I love you," you whisper. "Welcome home."

And you lay next to your wife in your room as it fills with sunshine.

Meanwhile, Ken stirs. You don't feel this because it's *that* insignificant, no noisier than a boisterous muffler on the opposite side of town. Your wife came home and all that Ken put into your head the past two days melts away in yet another gaze. You see clearly; you're staring into blue skies upon endless verdant fields, rolling; white picket fences cordoning off small pastures in which to raise and grow and to live for a while. You don't feel Ken when he tells you *She got a tattoo on her upper thigh,* and as a matter of fact, you won't give a shit when you discover this.

You sit up to put a breakfast on, and the kettle—

But Wifey says, “Stay for a while.” You thought she was sleeping.

“No!”

Wifey looks at you with wide eyes.

“Sorry, wasn’t talking to you,” you say before laying back into the sheets as you’re soon embraced in a hug as tight as you’ve ever experienced.

A hand cups your marblepouch and you look down to verify this startling occurrence—this equally unexpected treat.

Yup. Your wife is holding by the balls.

This is when you see the tattoo. You say, “Nice tattoo,” and then your wife says, “Thanks.”

“NO!”

There’s a pause, and then your wife says, “I assume you weren’t talking to me?”

“Absolutely not,” you say, and then:

Pump pump squirt.

NINE MONTHS LATER

Blanche

Acknowledgements

For a decade now my wife, Sam, has put up with such bullshit on my part that it boggles my mind she's stuck around. We have a daughter now, her name is Marlowe, and she's fucking amazing.

Sam, I thank you before all others. I love you and I am because you are.

Marlowe: you're four at the time of this publication and far from mature enough to read it but I hope one day you crack this thing open and get a couple laughs out of it, possibly even learn a thing or two about your old man, who is me—maybe I'll make a bit more sense to you. Never stop being you, even when you're too old to brazenly fart and to sniff them.

This book was for the two of you and if it weren't for the fun we've had over what time has been given to us (so far) never would Fatherhood for Fuckheads have ever been, so, thanks.

ABOUT THE AUTHOR

L.A. Dondo is the writer of online publications Fuckhead on Fatherhood and Regardless. Fatherhood for Fuckheads is his debut novel. He lives in Winnipeg, Canada, with his wife and daughter and they're his everything. You can find links to all of his work at www.dondowrites.com.

www.ingramcontent.com/pod-product-compliance
Lightning Source LLC
Chambersburg PA
CBHW060549310726
48982CB00008B/1062/J

* 9 7 8 1 7 3 9 0 0 5 8 0 1 *